SKY

A novelisation by Bob Baker

Adapted from the HTV series
by Bob Baker and Dave Martin

fantom
publishing

First published in 2015 by Fantom Films
fantomfilms.co.uk

A catalogue record for this book is available from the British Library.
Hardback edition ISBN: 978-1-78196-123-0

Typeset by Xanna Eve Chown
Jacket design by Stuart Manning

Printed and bound in the UK by CPI Group (UK) Ltd
Croydon, CR0 4YY

Contents

Preface   7

Chapter One   Burning Bright   17

Chapter Two   Countenance Divine   21

Chapter Three   Arby   25

Chapter Four   Dark Satanic Mills   57

Chapter Five   Goodchild   83

Chapter Six   What Dread Hand   103

Chapter Seven   And Did Those Feet?   127

Chapter Eight   Life Force   149

Chapter Nine   The Juganet   167

Chapter Ten   Chariot of Fire   173

Preface

NINETEEN SEVENTY FOUR had been a prolific time for Dave and I. Early in the year, we'd written four episodes of a children's adventure drama called *Ski Boy*. In addition, we wrote two episodes for the country copper series, *Hunter's Walk*. For HTV, we wrote two half-hour plays in the ITV Late Night Drama series: one called *Item,* the other *M&M,* the latter being a time-slip spoof on the quiz show *Mr and Mrs*. For ATV, we wrote an episode of the private eye series *Public Eye*. For the BBC, we did two episodes of the evergreen *Z Cars*, and just managed to squeeze in a *Doctor Who,* the two-parter *The Sontaran Experiment*.

Then, in the Autumn, HTV's Head of Programmes, Patrick Dromgoole, gave Dave Martin and me a commission:

'I want you to come up with a children's serial, of seven episodes.' Leonard White, who we'd worked with on an earlier children's serial, *Pretenders*, was to produce. And that was it. There was a slight 'and I want it by Friday' pressure about it too.

It's always nice to be given a clean sheet to start work on. I think we'd worked together with Patrick on so many projects from 1969 onward, that we were trusted to come up with something not just appropriate but perhaps controversial in some way. The only proviso for the ITV network was that, as usual, any story should centre around children and their families, for our nine-to-fourteen-year-old audience to identify with. Dave and I decided upon a science-fiction format, but contrary to our work on *Doctor Who*, with all its constrictions of budget, and *Doctor Who* provenance, we now had a chance to create our own time traveller. All we needed was a premise.

Looking back, what was 1974 like? What kind of world were Dave and I in, when we wrote *Sky*?

There were plenty of things going on which seemed punctuated at regular intervals by nuclear test blasts. One in the US, followed by one in Russia and vice versa – and in that year France too came into the nuclear equation.

In space matters, there was a lot going on. The US had a small orbiting small space station, Skylab, and the Russians had their own, Soyuz. That year too, an international message of 'Hello' was sent by radio telescope to the galaxy M41 2.500 light years away. (No reply as yet!) The Apollo programme was over, the space shuttle was on the cards.

So, on the one hand, we had the constant fear of nuclear war embedded in our minds, only to be compensated by exciting steps forward in the conquest of space, and greater and greater knowledge of the cosmos.

1974 was the year that Lord Lucan disappeared, President Nixon resigned over the Watergate affair, and the last *Monty Python* episode was screened. The Oscar for best movie was won by *The Sting*. Muhammad Ali KO'd George Foreman in the 'Rumble in the Jungle' World Championship fight. The World Trade Centre – the Twin Towers – had only just opened in New York…

A miners' strike caused the Three-Day Week and power cuts under Tory Ted Heath. A general election brought in Harold Wilson as Labour Prime Minister. The IRA were on the rampage in the Mainland Campaign – there was a bomb in a Guildford pub, a bus was blown up, and several people were killed and wounded.

In the arts, the novel of *Jaws* was published and became a bestseller in this year.

Around that time, there was a furore about UFOs – John Lennon claimed to have seen one in New York! There was a strong belief abroad that there were conspiracies by the government to cover-up sightings, landings and alien abduction.

Another best-selling book around that time, *Chariots of the Gods* by Erich Von Daniken, set out to suggest that our civilisation had been visited by aliens some time in the past, and that they had perhaps nurtured mankind – a concept used in Arthur C Clarke's *The Sentinel*, which Stanley Kubrick then made as the movie *2001: A Space Odyssey*.

Von Daniken sought evidence from various sources, including the Bible – in particular, the Book of Enoch – and the 'chariot of fire' there described sounded pretty convincing as a spaceship. He also cited ancient sculptures, such as those on Easter Island and Aztec reliefs, and suggested that they might depict images of spacemen. He then followed with that old argument: How could the Egyptians possibly build the pyramids, or the Druids Stonehenge, without help from an advanced civilisation?

However, when you came to analyse it, it would take a huge stretch of the imagination to see the Easter Island monoliths as spacemen. These possible beings would have needed to travel at least from another solar system some way off in our galaxy, and would inevitably been vastly superior to us in terms of intelligence… yet they all seemed to be wearing 1960s-type spacesuits!

Looking at that book now, the whole thing just seems so much nonsense, but in the Seventies we took it on board avidly. We wanted to believe it, and perhaps even *needed* to believe it, since there was hope, way, way, back in our minds, that these kindly aliens might return in time to help save us from ourselves.

We were in the midst of the Cold War, the East/West nuclear standoff. Also, around this time we were just beginning to understand the damage we were doing to the environment, such as the depletion of the ozone layer by the gasses used in fridges and aerosol cans – but the thought of doing something about carbon emissions was still something to be sorted out in the future.

So, Dave and I set up our time traveller, who was destined for a post-nuclear or ecological disaster Earth, where his brief would be to help the surviving inhabitants with his powers…

What we came up with had a bit of Von Daniken in the

sci-fi mix of a time traveller from a very advanced, but benign, civilization.

Other influential sources were *Planet Of The Apes* (1968), Robert A Heinlan's book *Stranger In A Strange Land, Logan's Run*, and the already mentioned *2001: A Space Odyssey*. In hindsight, *Sky* has a definite affinity with the – yet to be made – *E.T. the Extra Terrestrial* by Stephen Spielberg. Kids saving an alien being – yet another story nicked by S. Spielberg. (Not really!)

The other tub we wanted to thump was that of conservation and the increasing pollution all over the world, the devastation of the rainforests, the slow drip progress of dangerous and toxic substances getting into the oceans, all seen as wonderful additions to 'our modern lifestyle' as Wallace might say – but which could well threaten our very existence.

A month or so before starting to write this book, I was asked to contribute an idea for a TV serial. I wrote the following opening pitch.

In the very near future…

At a secret location somewhere in the Midwest of the USA, Driscoll, a Marine biologist, stands to address the delegates.

'Well, we've finally succeeded in bringing about our own demise by means of slow strangulation. The wanton destruction of rainforests, of wildlife…

Crops, which to grow more successfully are fed a dangerous cocktail of insecticides and growth boosters, are watered from drought-stricken rivers and precious deep aquifers. This is then washed into rivers along with fertilizer, dishwasher detritus, unnecessary bathroom chemicals, the remnants of antibiotics and the myriad other medical prescription drugs including the contraceptive pill. The polluted waters are flushed into the sewers and out to the sea. Ultimately this heavy pollution kills the fish that we eat and the very environment they live in.

I don't even need to mention the mad rush for fossil fuels, which in turn pollute the atmosphere. Well, ladies and gentlemen. On every front, the species called Homo Sapiens has finally reached the end of the line.

Oh, of course, it will get sorted out... in time. By intelligent reckoning it could be about five hundred thousand years, but it will mean the end of us... Man...

Some other species will climb to the top of the tree.'

Then, when I began the *Sky* novelisation, I was amazed by how similar the concepts were when I compared it to Sky's diatribes about the kind of people we had become, and the ruination of the planet by man. Have we, in fact, entered what Sky calls 'the Chaos'?

Sky was written in 1974! Sadly, despite forty-odd years having passed, fundamentally nothing much seems to have changed. Things have just chuntered on. Of course, there is more awareness of the danger now, but very little will is put into changing our ways. Things are now much worse, than they were then...

As for the characters, Dave and I felt that the children's drama area of television was still overly influenced by Fifties

Children's Hour thinking. The format was that children's drama should be treated differently to adult in terms of story scope and content.

There were still a few taboos, such as any children's story should, ideally, have the traditional family – that is mum, dad, boy and a girl. But by the mid-Seventies the so-called 'average family' was changing at an alarming rate. Divorce was easier and the so-called 'nuclear family' was beginning to fragment. Divorced and one-parent families were becoming fairly commonplace.

So Dave and I decided that we should take a chance on this and portray one of the children as from a one-parent family. There was also a gentle look at alcoholism in the character of Roy's dad, Major Briggs.

Some small surprises turn up, like the fact that the main characters, the Vennor family, do not have a telephone, but in the Seventies, not everyone did have a telephone… that was a fact. The majority of people either used the Post Office Red Box, or relied on asking a neighbour.

Also, that policemen ran country police stations, mostly rode bicycles, and the small patrol cars used mainly in cities, were called panda cars because of their blue and white two-tone livery. (But pandas aren't blue and white are they…?)

We were also aware of, and wanted to include, a sort of unbiased view of the various cults around at the time, like the hippies, astrology and the druids. So we chose to take a look at their beliefs and lifestyle, thus Glastonbury was brought into the mix, along with the kind of Arthurian myths and mysteries which we'd researched thoroughly when doing the series *Arthur Of The Britons*, also for HTV.

Dave and I found writing *Sky* very exciting and thoroughly enjoyable. Something that rekindled a tremendous enthusiasm in me when I started to go through it again.

Bob Baker
December 2014

Tiger, tiger, burning bright
In the forests of the night,
What immortal hand or eye
Could frame thy fearful symmetry?

from *The Tiger* by William Blake

Chapter One
'Burning Bright'

THE COSMOS.

A billion staring stars in the darkness of space and time… Through the emptiness came a small object… it was on a journey and carried with it a Traveller. The craft became seen clearly… it was like a slightly flattened ovoid shape… its surface was rough and pitted rather like an asteroid.

The Traveller was headed for a very specific time and place… he was to grow and evolve and mature during his long journey, as specified by those who sent him, so that on his arrival he would possess all the powers he would need to provide assistance to certain beings in some future time who found themselves in danger of extinction…

The Travellers had been in existence for nearly a million

Earth years. Their evolution had taken a very similar path to Man on Earth, and shared a similarity of physical structure, arms, legs, hands, feet.

It was in their brains that they differed. The Travellers had developed powers of the brain, with the same energetic zeal that the people of the Earth had shown in pursuing mechanics and technology, and built up a totally different source of power and energy, one that led away from using their world's resources as a means of dominating nature. For them, the way of travelling to distant planets was more a massive concentration of minds to propel their craft, rather than a wasteful display of physics, chemistry and hardware. By accommodating nature, retaining a balance between need and exploitation, the Travellers evolved a philosophy that nurtured the development of the mind – one worth, they believed, exporting to other worlds. Their occasional visits to other planets did not require conquest and death and possession of an empire. The Traveller's mission was to give species similar to their own no more than a gentle nudge in the right direction. Through time there had been many successes… and sadly, some failures, people who had lost their way and who needed a slight adjustment.

The Mission.

The flattened egg-shape capsule, which carried the Traveller, resembled an egg in another way. When the voyage began, the being inside the capsule had been little more than an embryo, so the pod contained all the means of supplying food, nourishment and growth for the occupant on his long journey, which might take years. On this long journey, the Traveller would have time in which to grow and mature, so that by the time of his arrival he would be perfectly formed, equipped and ready to carry out the task assigned to him.

The capsule looked like a tiny spot of light as it progressed serenely across the dark background of deep space. It maintained a steady course on its journey across the galaxy. The course had been set… All was well…

In the silence of dark space, there came a blinding flash of light. By sheer chance, something totally unpredictable had occurred. A nearby star had collapsed and gone supernova, and this star was close enough to cause the Traveller drastic problems. The shock waves emanating from the doomed star spread out like ripples of a stone thrown into a pool. Silent waves of sheer cosmic energy streamed out across space.

When the first wave reached the Traveller's path, his craft was tossed around like a canoe in a tsunami, helpless in the wild force released by the exploding star. Consequently, the tiny craft was thrown way, way, off its intended course…

The Being Inside.

The calm, sleeping Traveller had little knowledge of what had befallen him and was blissfully unaware that, because of the unforeseen cosmic event, the laws of gravity, time and relativity now came into play, laws which would irrevocably change his carefully pre-determined course to a specific time and destination…

The craft travelled on, the strange ship settled on a new course which eventually took it close to a brilliant sun. It then became influenced by the gravitational pull of the third planet in that solar system, a place of light blue oceans, with swirling white cloud above and colourful land masses...

It was on this world the Traveller made his intended landfall, in the year known there as 1974 AD.

Chapter Two
'Countenance Divine'

NO-ONE SAW THE LIGHT that descended into Hanham Woods that night. It glowed for a few seconds; it changed from white to orange, then blue and then was extinguished… Darkness again.

The Traveller, who was called Sky, had been deposited in woodland on a dark and damp November night. The woodland itself and all organic life around the craft greeted Sky's arrival with sudden mayhem, as if nature itself was reacting, with a raging anger, against this alien imposter. Winds blew up and came from all directions and quickly rose to gale force, then into a maelstrom that whipped the freshly fallen Autumn leaves into a swirling tornado-like cone. Trees bent and creaked, twigs snapped and flew off like arrows in the gale, all in an apparent effort to confront and unsettle the unwelcome newcomer.

The capsule opened up to reveal… the Traveller, Sky. He was unclothed but for a coating of a fluffy, sticky, organic substance attached to his body, which made him look rather like a fledgling bird that had just emerged from its egg.

The capsule he'd stepped from then melted away around him, into a watery substance that was absorbed by the ground… There was nothing left of it.

Sky was humanoid and in the form of a young and very beautiful young man, quite striking in appearance. He had tousled long blond hair and differed from ordinary humans only by his bulbous deep blue eyes that were seemingly without pupils.

Sky, a Traveller, one of the ones sometimes called 'The Most High' stood on a hillside in the strong wind… He faced toward the immediate area of woodland and raised his arms as if in a greeting to his new surroundings. Sky looked around at the world he'd been sent to and wondered why he'd not been greeted. In fact, he began to feel that something was amiss, that something had gone awry…

He put his hands over his eyes and concentrated his mind. It took only a short while to gather the information he needed to appraise his situation. He ran over the stored memory of events on his long journey, and realised that he had arrived in the wrong place… and the wrong time…

He moved his hands from his eyes and looked around at what he now knew was a hostile world. He received notice of that hostility when a most severe wind blew up, which bent the trees until it seemed they might snap under its force. Sky felt weak, he knew something was wrong and knew he could not muster enough strength to resist attack by the hostile world he'd entered. He slumped down on the ground, exhausted. His frail body began to be covered by the organic life around him. Leaves and twigs, blown by the strange, unearthly wind, built up around him and covered him completely as if he had a tomb of leaves…

The trees around him, straining in the gale, shed even more of their leaves and seemed to nod in howling wind-blown approval as Sky was gradually engulfed in the dank mulch of the woodland floor.

Chapter Three
'Arby'

THE SLOPES THAT RUN DOWN to the Bristol Avon between Bath and Bristol are, for the most part, pasture for dairy herds, but one privately owned stretch had been left entirely to woodland. It followed the curve of the river as it snaked its way towards the small town of Keynsham.

Part of the wood had been given over to pheasant breeding and, in season, was open for shooting parties, which were arranged by the local gun club.

The pheasant-shooting season had opened on this damp and dull Autumn Saturday. The ground was carpeted in fallen brown and ochre leaves. Everywhere the ground was a quagmire, all slippery and soggy underfoot after almost a fortnight of rain. The grey gloom was somewhat relieved by the chirping of birds making alarm calls. Deep in the wood, there was an atmosphere of danger. A pheasant's black eye stared out from a tangle of bracken, on the alert. Elsewhere in the woods, other creatures – a fox, deer and rabbits – seemed troubled and on edge, as if something sinister was about to happen…

The woods suddenly became silent.

That silence was broken by a strange tap-tapping sound… gradually building until it was identifiable as the rhythmic thwacking of sticks against tree trunks and bushes. The tapping sound came closer, then came the sound of human voices…

'Keep it uyp!'

'This way!'

'H-up!

A straggling line of beaters emerged from the trees, composed of local people of all ages. They'd been recruited to frighten the pheasants out of cover towards a line of waiting shooters, so that as the pheasants emerged from the woodland, their only way of escape was to take to their wings. Not a pheasant's best means of getting around. Rather like a chicken, their flight was more of a high, wildly flapping, extended jump over a fairly short distance, no more than fifty yards. This made them vulnerable as they rose out of the undergrowth right over a line of waiting sportsmen in order to be shot at and downed by their guns.

The chief beater, a young farmer in green wellies, checked waistcoat and a flat cap, blew on an antique silver whistle for his line to make another advance.

'On me!' he shouted.

Several birds scuttled through the undergrowth. The chief beater's springer spaniel, mysteriously called No Biting, became over-excited and started springing – as was its wont. The dog tried to break free to chase the birds and was restrained by a tug on his lead from the beater. He then looked up at his master, 'crying' as if begging to be forgiven, and to show how keen he was to be ordered to fetch when a bird was downed.

'No! No Biting! Down boy,' said his master, turning and shouting to his beaters. 'Come on! Keep in line there! On me!'

Outside the wood, on a sloping grassy field, stood the line of shooters from the South Gloucestershire Shooting Club. They had their twelve-bore shotguns at the ready for when the pheasants were flushed out by the beaters. Suddenly, several pheasants made their ungainly flight out of the wood. The shooters let off a volley and downed a couple of them.

In the wood, the beaters moved forward again, now making whooping cries. The chief beater blew his whistle again. Another line of shooters took up their positions as the first ones were reloading. Among the new line-up was a blond-haired young man, Roy, who seemed to be almost dwarfed by the shotgun he was aiming. Unlike any of the other guns, who were in heavy-duty tweed jackets with waistcoats, plus fours and gum-boots, Roy was wearing a trendy, short, shiny Italian leather jacket, a brightly striped jumper and flared trousers.

Several more pheasants made erratic flights out of the wood. Roy aimed his shotgun and fired at one. And hit it – apparently…

Roy's father, Major Briggs, a retired army officer who'd taken living in the countryside to heart, looked very countrified in his deerstalker hat, tweed suit, yellow cravat and de rigueur green wellies.

He turned to Roy and spoke in a rather strained, clipped upper-class tone. 'Good shooting there, lad? Good boy, good shooting!' Then, as he passed a fellow shooter, he laughed and remarked, 'I miss 'em, he gets 'em, eh?'

This was meant to be a verbal pat-on-the-back, but Roy was not particularly demonstrative toward his father, and greeted the 'compliment' with a flat smile and a curt nod, then moved away.

A Land Rover was parked in the field near the shoot. A young man was watching the proceedings carefully. His name was Arby, Arby Vennor.

Arby? Oh, the name came about because when he was at junior school, a certain American TV cartoon show was very popular. It was called *Top Cat*. The main character, a very cool cat, was known by all as TC. So, Arby and a few of his mates started calling themselves by their initials as a joke. Roger Brian Vennor became RB, or Arby, and the name stuck.

Arby was a wily local lad who'd volunteered, or rather snapped up, the job of going into the thicket after the shoot to search for and retrieve any downed birds that hadn't been collected by the dogs. He would take them to a nearby barn for distribution at the end of the shoot. For this, Arby looked forward to receiving a generous tip.

He was just seventeen, and had passed his driving test first time. Not too surprising, as he'd been allowed to drive around the farms and back lanes since he was fourteen, but a vehicle licence gave him a certain air of superiority, especially amongst his peers, and Arby just loved being seen driving his father's battered old Land Rover around the place.

Arby was clever – smart might be a better description. He was country-wise, in the same way as townies might be called 'streetwise'. He knew how to do a lot of things that could well be useful for what he saw as his future, one that would obviously be in some kind of rural occupation. Going into Bristol to find work in a shop or a factory, like many of his contemporaries had been doing in recent years, was definitely not for him. In many ways, Arby was one of the last of his kind, one of a dying breed, in that he was genuinely interested in the country, animals, their welfare and conservation. He'd been brought up in the country ways and he felt comfortable with them.

Arby held what were fast becoming very rare skills, such as how to snare and skin a rabbit, then cook and eat it. He knew how to fish the streams, and all the different kinds of fish, and he was an excellent shot too. His friends found such things unnecessary, messy and primitive, and preferred their radio and TV, pop songs and soap operas. Sometimes he was made fun of by older members of his peers, but they were jibes that Arby took with a smile. No way could he be put down. Arby was very confident and pretty proud of himself, and he didn't mind if it showed.

With Arby in the Land Rover was his sister, Jane. She was a year or so younger than Arby. She had strong features, with long auburn hair, and was wrapped up warm in a fleece jacket. She was looking over towards the gun line, keeping a surreptitious eye on Roy's performance. She had always been a bit of a tomboy and had lived a bit in Arby's shadow until now, but she was beginning to find her feet. Jane had an ambition. She wanted to assert herself and buck the trend of most of the young girls of her age. It seemed that, if they didn't just stay at home, waiting to get married and settle down, they chose secretarial, nursing, or shop work to fill in the time before getting engaged.

Jane had a dream. She would love to become some kind of skilled worker – an electrician, a plumber or perhaps, even better, an apprentice engineer – something that had always been the preserve of men, and was definitely seen as taboo for ladies. However now, albeit very slowly, things were beginning to change. But this was something Jane very much kept to herself. For now...

Meanwhile, she was holding another secret. She was rather taken by Roy, the newcomer to the village who'd moved in right next door. She found him to be refreshingly different from the rest of the lads around the place, but was careful to keep her feelings for him very much to herself.

Roy, elated by his efforts, rushed over to Arby and Jane looking for their approval. Roy punched the air.

'See that then, Arby?' he said.

'Well done!' said Jane.

All Arby did was make a face. He daren't show approval of Roy's feat. He felt he had to be seen as aloof, neutral and unimpressed, so as to maintain his position.

Who's he think he is? thought Arby. Him and his stuck-up father! They hadn't been in the village long, and now they seemed to think they owned it. Arby decided to put Roy in his place. 'You winged him, that's all.'

Roy noted Arby's superior stance. He knew Arby would want to rubbish his feat, but decided to let it go. And anyway, he was somehow duly compensated by Jane's warm smile and her tacit admiration for him.

Arby had noticed the smile too, but didn't mention it. He secretly disapproved of it, since it affected his relationship with Jane, but because it was about emotions he couldn't put it into words. He was wary of all this soppy 'love' thing. It was something he felt totally unable to deal with.

Roy Briggs was academically more intelligent than Arby. He'd lived most of his life in London and displayed a definite estuarial twang to his voice. Roy had been brought up by his mother in Crystal Palace, South London. His dad was always abroad – Libya, Germany, then Cyprus – he was an officer in the Royal Army Pay Corps and was in charge of a lot of Her Majesty's money. But Roy's mother had refused to let Roy become a camp-following army brat, pushed from pillar to post around different schools all over the world. She was adamant that the boy had some kind of continuity to his education. Or that was the way she'd explained it to Roy, but now he'd begun to wonder if there had been something more to it than that…

So, for fourteen years of his life, Roy lived with his mother, with only the occasional visit from his father. Then tragedy. Roy's mother died suddenly, and totally unexpectedly, from a massive heart attack. She'd been singing in the local choir and, as it was put to Roy by a family friend, she was on a high note when she literally dropped dead. She went on to tell him how it was merciful to pass away without pain or long illness – as if that would help. This had been a painful time for Roy, but he knew he had to get on with his life.

Then came another shock. His father, a virtual stranger, was now coming back to take over the household.

His father took early retirement from the forces with the rank of Major, to take up the reins of the family. He felt that the best way for Roy to 'get over' his mother was to move. The Major felt the West Country would be ideal, as he'd been stationed there during his service. He eventually settled for a small village near Bath, and a distraught Roy found himself dragged away from his school, his friends and the metropolis, to a life in the wilds of Gloucestershire. 'Scrumpyland' as Roy dubbed it when they first arrived. All this, and with a father who Roy found was quite distant, a man stuck in his ways. Not at all as liberal and forgiving as his mum had been. But Roy knew that his dad was trying, and knew that if he didn't try too, there would be nothing but misery to contend with until he left home at some future time.

Roy took some time to learn how to cope with his dad's old-fashioned ways, but after a while he realised that the simplest way of avoiding trouble was to remove the target – a simple military solution as it happened. Roy just had to lay low and keep out of his father's way as much as possible. And, in fact, the move to the 'Out West', as Roy described it, did help him sort himself out. It was new ground and, without realising it, knowing Arby and Jane had helped him too.

As for his dad, the Major had received a shock of nuclear proportions. He'd made a definite decision to 'do his duty' where Roy was concerned, but *how* to do it was something the poor man had some difficulty understanding. He admitted that he had no idea whatsoever how to accomplish it. Added to this, he suddenly found himself in – what he saw as – the mad, unordered world of the Seventies. Gone was the smooth running of army life, somewhere he'd been settled and happy. He'd thought that as long as you played by the rules, life could be one easy path to promotion, and a sizeable pension. Perfect.

So both Roy and his father were suffering from shock and both had their crosses to bear. However, Roy was resilient and good at appreciating when situations might lead to conflict. He was intelligent enough to deflect them without his father even realising it was happening. After just over a year together, he was beginning to understand how to manage life with his dad. All this, despite the fact that Roy himself was going through the natural teenage affliction of puberty, that inner rebellion, the desire to confront accepted social and even political mores and change things.

It was Roy's knack for appraising situations that led him to allow Arby to come on the way he did. He understood that Arby needed to play the 'Big I Am'. For the moment that was. Just until he and Roy got know each other better, then perhaps, they could decide whether to continue their friendship or simply put an end to it and go separate ways. For now, they were still sounding each other out and only close in that they lived next door to one other.

When the Briggs's moved in, Arby's mum, Joyce, had begged Arby and Jane to befriend their new neighbours – who were, to her mind, 'respectable people.'

Arby knew that she meant 'upper class' or 'gentry' or something. And that his mum had a kind of inbred forelock-tugging mentality when it came to class distinction. Not respect, but fear of the power assumed by these people. This was something Arby certainly hadn't inherited, however he'd agreed that he'd try. But for Arby there would be no kow-towing – it had to be on his terms. He had to prove his superiority to Roy and this would be in terms of the things Arby knew about. And that was country ways.

Jane had no such hang-up. Her attraction to Roy was immediate and quite enough for her. But of course, as always, she kept her private dreams strictly to herself.

As Roy stood beside the Land Rover next to Jane, Arby gave him a sour look. 'That poor bird's going to be crawling around that wood in agony till he dies.'

Roy's euphoria at his shooting gave way to concern.

Arby nodded toward the Land Rover. 'Better go and find it… Get in then,' he said with a smirk.

A slightly chastened Roy scrambled into the vehicle and sat next to Jane. He was not quite sure if Arby was right or not, but he let it seem that he was.

Jane pointed to where she thought she saw the bird drop. 'It went down the in the copse, over there.'

Arby frowned. 'I got eyes.'

Roy smiled at Jane. 'Your brother always talk to you like that?'

Jane was flattered by Roy taking her side. She smiled, basking in Roy's support, turned to her brother and decided to back Roy. 'Who shot it anyway?'

'Your friend – maimed it,' retorted Arby.

Then he imitated Roy's father's voice. 'Well shot lad!'

Roy didn't react. He felt pretty embarrassed by his dad anyway, and decided to change the subject. 'Let's have some heat, shall we?' He grabbed at the heater knob and it came off in his hand.

Arby shook his head and sighed. 'Brilliant…'

Jane swiftly took the heater knob from Roy. This was her chance to impress him. 'Don't worry, Roy, I'll get that mended later on,' she said brightly.

Arby drove out past the shooters to go in search of the wounded bird. The Land Rover slithered over the damp grass as Arby tried to get as close as possible to the spot where the bird fell. The vehicle started up a slope and Arby got up as far as he could, but not even the Land Rover's four-wheel drive could make it go up any further.

Arby and Roy got out.

'You coming, Jane?' said Arby.

She was inspecting the heater control, deciding how to fix the knob back on. 'No. I'll get this sorted out,' she said.

Arby took charge and directed Roy to his area of the search. 'You go right,' he said.

'Fine,' replied Roy.

'Shout out if you find it. I'll put it out of its agony.'

'OK, OK, don't worry,' returned Roy, and they moved off into the woods.

Arby pushed his way through a patch of briar and found himself on a muddy track that dipped away into a dense stand of larger trees. He felt absolutely sure he would find the bird, and sauntered along the path up to a ridge.

As he reached the treeline at the top, he became aware of

a sudden fierce wind that seemed to come from nowhere. The trees around him were bending and the wind made a whooshing sound. Arby looked around with some concern. Where the hell did that come from? he wondered to himself. It was so unexpected that Arby – even Arby – began to feel a tiny bit frightened... He moved on but kept a wary eye open for... something... What?

Arby noticed that other creatures were being affected. He caught sight of a fox speeding past, and then a stag ran quite close to him as it ran away from the strange wind. He wondered why the animal had run towards him. That was very unusual. They were usually so skittish, and it ran straight past him. No fear at all, it just ran.

Arby plodded on, and then slipped down from the top of the ridge on the other side. He got up and picked up a stick, using it to help him climb the other slope.

He then heard something...

It was a voice... whispering to him.

He swung around to see who it might be, then realised, to his horror, that the voice was in his head.

'Help me!' cried the voice. It had the air of an imperative about it.

Arby felt that the whole atmosphere of the woods had changed. The flora he'd been familiar with for years now took on a sinister aspect as it blew in the wind...

He moved on a few more steps, then stopped. He looked down at something on the slope just in front of him. He frowned, and wondered just what the hell it might be. It was a pile of leaves, which, when he looked closer, seemed to move slightly. Was it the wind? Whatever it was, it raised the hairs on the back of his neck.

To overcome his fear, he knew he had to investigate further, and dispel any ghostly thoughts. So, despite feeling decidedly scared, and with the dread of finding a decomposing body or something, Arby felt impelled to go toward the heap of leaves. As he came close to the leaf pile, Arby used the stick he'd found to move some of the leaves. It was then he saw movement again…

He decided to uncover whatever it was. Discarding his stick, he used his hands, and as he pulled a bunch of leaves away, a pale hand came out from the leaf pile and grabbed his wrist!

Arby looked on in utter horror and amazement as a leaf-covered head slowly protruded from the mound, and the leaves fell away to reveal the face of a young man with weird dark blue eyes – which fixed Arby in a stare that completely mesmerised him…

'Yaaaa!' shouted Roy, causing Jane to scream with fright.

She appeared to be being attacked by some horrible feathered creature through the open window of the Land Rover. But she quickly realised it was Roy, having a bit of fun with his dead pheasant, pushing it through the window trying to scare her!

Getting over the initial shock, Roy started laughing at his successful bit of fun.

'Do you have to?' yelled Jane.

Roy he could tell she didn't really mind. 'It's alright, it's dead. Your brother was wrong for once.'

Jane tried to be blasé and turned her attention to repairing the heater. She was trying to use a nail file as a screwdriver.

'Where is he anyway? Taking long enough isn't he?' she said, as she looked out of the cab window.

Roy sniggered. 'Still out there looking for it.' He was highly amused to have beaten Arby to it, but it was a hollow victory if Arby wasn't there. Roy peep-peeped the horn, but there was no response…

Then suddenly, Arby came scrambling out through the trees in one hell of a hurry. He was frantic about something, and hustled them out of the Land Rover.

'Out you get, I need it. You'll have to walk back down. I need the Land Rover,' he said.

'What for?' said Jane.

'Never mind what for!' Arby replied with some force.

'Can't we come?' pleaded Roy.

Arby realised he was making them suspicious and softened his tone. 'No, not really.'

Jane got out reluctantly, but stood her ground. Hands on hips she issued a warning. 'If you get into trouble again…'

But the noise of the revving engine drowned her threat.

Roy yelled at Arby. 'Hey, Arby what about the birds? You're supposed to get them back to the farm!'

'Don't worry I'll be there!' Arby shouted back.

Roy and Jane watched him drive off.

'What was all that about?' said Roy.

'He's found something,' said Jane with a knowing look.

Roy frowned. 'What?'

Jane considered for a second whether or not she should tell Roy, but decided to make him her confidant and share some of her secrets.

'It were copper wire last time… dumped.'

This brought a smile to Roy's face. 'Oh, *nicked*, you mean?'

Jane became defensive. 'Arby didn't pinch it. Just... found it, that's all.'

'Oh yeah,' smiled Roy.

Jane marched off down the hill, turned and gave him a conspiratorial smile, then called back at Roy. 'Got a caution though.'

Roy appreciated Jane's information about Arby, and returned her smile with a grin. He began to think, as he followed her back down toward the shooters, that he'd found a good ally in Jane. Considering all things, he was beginning to get quite fond of her, but strictly on a friendly basis of course... for now.

Arby rushed through the heaps of leaves, carrying a large airforce greatcoat towards the spot where he'd seen the strange figure. When he reached it, there was nobody there... Arby looked around the place, unsure if he might have imagined the whole thing.

I know he was here, thought Arby. Where's he gone?

He decided to get back to the Land Rover. He scrambled over the ridge and opened the door to shove the overcoat in. To his shock and surprise, he found the strange figure sitting there in the lotus position, staring straight at him.

Again, Arby heard the voice in his head.

'Stranger... I am called Sky... You must keep me away from living things.'

Arby knew, for some unexplained reason, that he had no choice but to comply with the voice. Even though he wrestled with the thoughts he was having, he found himself carrying out Sky's orders. He got into the Land Rover and drove off, wheels skidding in the soft mud. The car went into a lane, then across a field and entered a sort of mini gorge. It was a disused railway cutting, the remains of a colliery dram line, which led to a tunnel. The steep sidewalls began to darken and narrow as they approached the tunnel, which took the old line beneath a steep hillside on its way down to the river landing stage about a mile away.

This was Arby's secret place...

Arby felt sure the stranger would be safe in his hideaway. When he reached the tunnel entrance, Arby got out and moved toward the arch, which was overgrown with ivy and new saplings. Bushes grew each side of it, making it practically invisible if you didn't know it was there. The opening was blocked off by planks of timber. Arby pulled two of them aside and looked in, and yet again he was spooked by swirling zephyr-like winds that blew the leaf carpet at the tunnel entrance up in flurries.

Arby went inside the tunnel and looked around to satisfy himself that no-one had been there... All was as it should be. Arby then he moved to his 'lair', where he had made himself a little alcove hidey-hole. There was a mattress on the ground, broken furniture and some wooden boxes filled with junk, all hidden behind a screen of rusted sheets of corrugated iron roofing. Again, Arby was satisfied that his 'place' hadn't been used by a tramp or discovered by some other kids. He felt it was ready to receive his new acquaintance. So he turned to go and get Sky, but again, to his amazement he found him standing face to face in front of him...

Sky was now wearing the bulky, ill-fitting greatcoat. He

took in his surroundings, the arched brickwork of the tunnel the damp floor.

'What is this place?' said Sky, in Arby's head.

'Oh, it's a tunnel for an old dram line, when the trucks used to go down to the river to unload their coal into barges... Long time ago that was. I use it as somewhere I can put things, sort of private like.'

Arby could hardly see Sky in the gloom of the tunnel. He was nervous too, but decided to cover his fear by getting some light in the place. Arby was shaking as he fiddled with the matches and lit an old oil lamp. He raised the light to look around, and again he saw that Sky had mysteriously moved and was now sitting in the lotus position on the mattress in front of him.

Again Sky's voice whispered in his head. 'Good place... safe here... heal now.'

Arby just stared at him, at those unearthly cobalt blue eyes, with lids that never seemed to close. They really put Arby on edge. Then, the sound of an eerie moaning wind chilled him even more. A few leaves in the tunnel were agitated and fluttered around. Arby looked behind him to see that the entrance had now sealed over. The metal sheets had re-arranged themselves to form a curtain, cutting them off from the tunnel entrance.

'Here, what's goin' on? How did that happen?' said Arby, choking back his fear.

The stranger raised his head and spat out the word, 'Juganet!' He now spoke with his mouth, but his speech was faltering, as if he had just learned the language.

'What?' said Arby cautiously.

'The... Juganet. Where is it?'

'What?' said Arby, utterly at a loss.

Sky bowed his head and considered the situation, then looked up at Arby again. He began to think that something had gone very wrong with his journey. It was obviously worse than he had at first imagined. He badly needed information.

'What time is this? What time is this? There is danger!'

The howling wind started up again. Sky leapt to his feet.

'Answer me!' shouted Sky.

Arby was terrified for a moment, but recovered and tried to calm him down. 'Now hold on, stay where you are. You want something?' Thinking that Sky was in some kind of pain because of his eyes, Arby gestured toward his own. 'If you want somethin' for it… your eyes, I'll get someone.'

Sky held Arby fixed with his staring eyes. Like a rabbit in a headlight beam. 'You are frightened. Why are you frightened?'

'Because, well, I don't know who are you?' Arby blurted.

'Do you not know me?' Sky was genuinely taken aback.

There were sounds coming from outside, Arby turned to go to the door.

This produced a sharp, 'No!' from the stranger. 'No-one must know I am here.'

Arby still backed away, but Sky raised his hand and thrust it toward him. Arby was stopped in his tracks, as if held by something.

Sky's eyes were like windows into the darkness of space and the universe invisible force. Sky's blue eyes now turned to black… then beyond…

Sally-On-The-Barn was a twelfth century tithe barn with a

gothic statue of Saint Sarah, the patron saint of the Romany people, on the top. It was very much a landmark in the area. It was thought to have once been part of extensive monastery farm buildings for the nearby Hanham Abbots – yet another of the monasteries that Henry VIII ruined. It was, of course, thought to be haunted. 'Sally' was sometimes seen crossing the nearby fields at night enveloped in a silvery glow…

The shooting party which, including Major Briggs, were waiting beneath the statue, were partaking of liquid refreshments. They were getting a bit impatient too, worried about when they might collect the rest of their birds.

'Where the devil is that lad?' shouted one of the guns.

'Can't be that damn difficult for him, surely?' moaned another.

Briggs looked out at the fields beyond, but there was no sign of Arby.

Another one of them addressed the Major. 'Come on, Major, I've got to get back!' he said irritably.

Roy was standing with his father, who took a sip from a hip flask before making an announcement. 'Sorry about the wait. You'll get your birds alright. It's, ah, the young feller looking after the birds is a bit of a tearaway you know… Only gets into a bit of minor trouble, isn't that right, Roy?'

Murmurs of anger and annoyance came from the gun club members as Roy stalked off, not wishing to be brought into anything. He felt a little embarrassed by his father, who was slurring his words a bit.

The Major called to him, 'Roy!'

Without turning, Roy anticipated the question.

'I'm going to look for Arby, Dad. OK?'

The Major went after him, grabbed him by the arm, and hissed, 'He's ruined the shoot you know!'

'Don't take it out on me because your friends are upset.'

The Major was ruing the day he'd asked Arby to do the job of collecting the birds. Just goes to show, he thought to himself. You try and be helpful and friendly and you get this! Obstruction and embarrassment of the first order!

Then, trying to placate Roy, he said, 'Look. All I'm asking from you is a little cooperation.'

'I'm going to look for him, aren't I?'

'He's probably sold the lot by now.'

Roy stopped. Whatever he felt about Arby, suggesting – without any evidence – that Arby was on the take was a bit much. Roy decided to stop his father in his tracks. He turned to face his father. 'Dad, why not have another drink… OK?'

The Major looked hurt and slightly guilty. He was about to make a remark, but turned away and left.

As Roy walked past Jane towards his motorbike, he winked at her and said, 'You coming?'

She gave a broad smile and said, 'Thought you'd never ask.'

She sat astride the pillion seat of Roy's 250cc trials type motorbike. Roy turned the key and started it up. Then off they went. Jane was quietly elated and dared to hold on tight around Roy's waist.

Roy and Jane searched the lanes where Arby had left them, but couldn't find anything. They tried old farm tracks and then got out on to the roads again. Still nothing.

Roy began to think that Arby really had gone off with the birds. He stopped and turned to Jane. 'Where the hell's he got to? Any ideas?'

Jane thought for a second and then decided. 'Yes, I think I know where he is, but –'

'What? Come on, my dad's going potty back there.'

'Well I shouldn't – I mean Arby said he kill me if I was to tell anyone.'

Roy decided to turn on the charm. He turned to her and looked deep into her eyes. 'Tell me, can't you?'

He broke out in a confident grin, bordering on sexy, and she melted. She pointed to a clump of trees up ahead.

'Alright then… Up there on the left, there's a stone gatepost just past those trees. Turn in there.'

Roy revved the bike up and drove towards the trees.

In the tunnel, Arby was now so frightened of Sky that had taken up a wooden stake to defend himself and was holding it like a baseball bat.

'I'm warning you.'

Sky turned to him slowly and in faltering voice said, 'You do not understand?'

Sky had not wanted to freak Arby out and, thinking he would ease things by giving him a getaway, he willed the metal sheet to open again.

Arby noticed the tunnel was open and duly made another effort to escape, backing slowly away. 'How'd that happen?'

'You… were afraid… you… panicked,' replied Sky.

Arby relaxed a bit and lowered the stick.

Sky shook his head in disbelief. 'You… really do not know me… Do you? What… time is this?'

Arby, misunderstanding, said, 'About half past eleven.'

'Yes?' Sky urged for more information.

'Saturday. Saturday, the 15th.'

'The 15th?'

'Yes, November 15th, 1974.'

'Nineteen hundred and seventy four?' Four what?' quizzed Sky.

'Years. That's the date.'

Sky leaned towards him. 'Before or after the Chaos?'

'What chaos?' Arby answered, frowning.

'Then you are Before... So you were not mind-blocking? You have no telepathic facility... Then this must be... the Decline!'

It suddenly dawned on Sky. He was sure now that, whilst he was on his journey, something must have swept him onto a new trajectory. One that had caused him to arrive, he calculated, about a hundred Earth years too early...

'Eh? I don't know what you're on about. What chaos?' Arby was still very confused. He studied Sky, who was now deep in thought.

'I thought you were expecting me... It is worse then... Listen, there is a force against me. A force generated by my arrival... It is growing, increasing in strength... I must be gone before it becomes... manifest... Now, tell me. Where is it? Where is the Juganet?'

Arby began to think he was with a complete nutcase. He must be mad. Escaped from a mental asylum or something. Having convinced himself, Arby tried, as best as he could, to be gentle with him. 'Hey,' he said. 'They take away your clothes, did they? Where you came from?'

Sky crossed him sharply. 'Listen! The Juganet is a circle,

the circle is a machine, the machine is a crossover point, the point is a paramagnetic interception. That is where I must be... Not here.'

Arby was still thoroughly confused. He had never, ever heard of such a thing as a Juganet. He stood up as if to go. 'Right. Tell you what. I'll get you somebody, shall I? Someone who knows about – er – that what you just said?'

He started backing away.

Sky was now showing signs of frustration. 'No! This is unbelievable! You must know. There have always been such machines. They were placed here for the Travellers. You must know?'

Arby was now absolutely petrified and continued backing away. 'Yes, I'll get somebody who – uh – does that. Now you stay where you are. Alright?

Sky rose to his feet and held the flat palm of his hand towards Arby, who froze like a statue, as if paralysed.

'Come here,' ordered Sky.

Arby obediently turned and marched zombie-like toward Sky, staring deep into Sky's window-on-the-universe eyes, transfixed by what he saw there.

Jane was on Roy's motorbike, and loving it. They passed the stone gatepost and went along a track.

She pointed out a stony path and shouted above the engine noise, 'Over there! It's an old railway line.'

Roy looked down the long narrow cutting then turned into it. They drove on toward the tunnel entrance.

'Yes. That's it!'

Jane directed Roy to go into the cutting.

'Are you sure? Down there?' he shouted.

'Yes. Go on! You'll be surprised. There's a tunnel!'

Roy carried on, dodging the stones and trying to keep to the rutted wheel marks. When they approached the tunnel entrance they saw the Land Rover parked up. Jane hopped off quickly, then rushed ahead of Roy and looked at the boards in front of the tunnel entrance with a satisfied smile. She knew that's where he'd be! She also knew that Arby would be mad at her for coming, but somehow she didn't care.

Roy, on his way to join her, decided to check inside the Land Rover for the birds. 'Well, the birds are all there…' he said, and then ran to catch her up. 'So where's Arby?'

'In there,' she nodded towards the tunnel.

Inside the tunnel, Arby was being subjected to Sky's powers as he conducted a painful-looking mind scan. Sky was concentrating hard as Arby moaned and groaned under the pressure of it. He was then released.

Arby rubbed his head. 'Oowww! What did you do?'

Sky sounded resigned and spoke calmly. 'I had to search your mind… I did not expect to find something so… primitive… so confused. Because you cannot understand, you think I am insane…'

Arby revived his spirit. 'Yeah, right, well what d'you expect? I don't know anythin' about you. How am I to know if you're telling me the truth?

'Listen to me… Arby… I am not from this time. I am a Traveller… there was an… accident…'

'Accident?' Arby frowned and went on. 'What sort of accident?'

'It would be difficult for you to comprehend… Suppose

an unripe seed falls into a stream. It cannot germinate…
it cannot fulfill its purpose. It then finds itself in an alien
world, like a shipwrecked voyager, a stranger in a strange
land.'

Arby tried hard to keep up with Sky's simile. He picked
up on the shipwreck image, and remembered something
from his childhood: an illustrated book, showing a giant
Gulliver pulling the Lilliputian navy into port.

'Like Gulliver you mean?'

'Who?'

'In Lilliput. *Gulliver's Travels.*' Arby tried to be relaxed. He
casually opened a can of Coke and took a sip.

Sky did not recognise the Gulliver allusion. 'Many
Travellers have visited this planet.'

Arby offered the can to Sky. Sky did not respond. Then,
Arby felt a bit over-confident and went way beyond the
mark as he said with an amused sneer. 'So, you from outer
space or something? Where's your flying saucer then?'

Sky shook his head slowly. 'If you could use more than half
your brain. If it were not just a series of disconnected cul-
de-sacs, such a squalid, primitive, emotional junkyard…'
Sky stared hard at Arby. 'There is no ship, Arby. Not as you
understand it. Energy is not always created by physical
means.'

Arby was duly chastened, and began to show some
sympathy for the strange being he'd discovered. 'What you
gonna do then?'

'The Juganet. I must find the Juganet.'

Jane and Roy entered the tunnel through the planks, Jane
showing the way,

'Come on. He keeps all his bits and bobs in here,' she confided.

'Things he's nicked you mean?' said Roy.

'That's the trouble with you and your dad. He's not a criminal you know.'

'Alright, I'm sorry.'

'Don't jump to bloody conclusions then.'

Roy smiled to himself at having got a reaction from Jane. He then started to look around in the dark, dank tunnel. He was not at all impressed. 'I suppose he thinks he's clever,' he mused. 'Who's he think he is? Ali Baba? Open Sesame!'

Jane hadn't quite caught Roy's clever remark and didn't react this time. She was too concerned about how Arby would feel about her intrusion into his business.

She cautiously moved further into the tunnel. 'What did you say?

'Oh nothing.' Roy slowed up and looked around at the bits and pieces that Arby had ferreted away in this dump.

'You comin' or not?'

Sky was seated again.

Arby was pleading with him. 'I don't know what this Juganet thing is, do I? Never heard of it. How am I supposed to find it?'

'You will find the Juganet… because it exists,' insisted Sky.

Arby saw this as an out, as a way to get away from Sky. He moved toward him slowly. 'You, ah… you'll let me go then? I'll find out where this… thing is and I'll come back and let you know… shall I?'

Since Sky made no attempt to stop him, Arby turned to

go. But just as he was about to leave, Sky again rose up and focused his sinister eyes on Arby.

Sky called after him, in a commanding voice in his head again, 'You will tell no-one I am here. Secret-t-t-t-t-'

The word echoed in the tunnel... and the voice was in Arby's head. Yet again, he was mesmerised by it. 'Yeah... that's alright. Secret... I promise.'

As he came to, he started for the way out. He got a shock when Jane poked her head through the opening.

She was puzzled by Arby's scared look. 'Arby?'

'Eh?' said Arby. His first reaction was to turn toward Sky, but there was no sign of him. The mattress he'd been sitting on was empty. For a brief second he thought perhaps it had all been a dream, an illusion... Then Arby was himself again. He turned to Jane irritably. 'What d'you want? Haven't I told you? You're not to come here. This is my place!'

To Arby's surprise and consternation, she just smiled confidently. 'Oh, you're for it, Arby. They're all going mad back at the barn. We came out to find you,' she said with a superior look on her face.

Arby's face was set in anger and indignation. 'I've told you, you wasn't to come 'ere. Didn't I?'

Jane started to look around. She was very suspicious. He must have been hiding something, probably something he shouldn't have. She knew Arby too well. 'What are you up to Arby? What've you got in here?' She tried to go past him, further into the tunnel, but he blocked her way. 'What you doin' in here, Arby?'

Arby pushed her back and then noticed Roy. He made a face. 'Oh no. What d'you bring him for?'

'They all think you nicked their pheasants,' said Roy.

'Yeah, they would, wouldn't they,' said Arby, resigned.

Jane made another move to see into the cavern. Again Arby put himself between her and the cavern. 'Come on, Arby. What've you got in there?'

'Mind your own,' snapped Arby, and pushed her quite roughly back through the opening. 'Shove off!'

'No need to get physical,' warned Jane.

'Well I wouldn't have to if you'd just move! Come on, both of you. Out!' He bundled them both out toward the tunnel entrance…

Sky appeared again above the mattress, floating in his lotus position. He was staring at the departing trio…

Outside, at the tunnel entrance, Jane fell as she was bundled out by Arby. He was still angry with them.

Roy put himself between Arby and Jane. 'Come on, that's enough Arby, no need for that –'

'Don't come sniffin' around here again… Come on.' He led them back to the Land Rover.

Inside the tunnel, Sky, alone and vulnerable, knew that it wouldn't be long before the Animus, the earthly force of nature, would try to attack and destroy him once more. He also understood that it was he who was totally at fault, and he bore no malice toward this time and place. However, he had a mission to perform in a future time and that held precedence. He must complete his mission if it was at all possible. For the moment he felt reasonably safe, in a place where he could allow his powers to generate to the full, but for that he would need to conserve his strength as much as possible.

Though, when Sky surveyed his surroundings more closely, he became a little worried about the fact that there were some places in the brick-lined tunnel where the roots of plants and trees up above had, over the previous two hundred years of disuse, pushed their way out through into the tunnel…

Sky watched in alarm, as a tree root suddenly began to writhe and twist, then slowly began to creep towards him… He was helpless as more snake-like roots joined in a slow, but relentless movement to attack and gradually entwine him…

The kids reached the Land Rover. Roy turned to Jane hopefully. 'Coming with me?'

'No thanks, I'll take the Land Rover.'

She got in beside Arby, determined to find out what her brother was up to.

Once Roy had gone off on his motorbike, Jane decided to tackle Arby, who was angrily crashing the gears as he manoeuvred between the boulders in the cutting. She was puzzled by his rage.

'What have you been up to Arby? What is it you found? Come on Arby, you can tell me.'

'Something,' was his sullen answer.

'What though?'

'I can't tell you, that's all… It's not something I wanted. I can tell you that!'

Jane frowned. 'What?'

At the tunnel entrance, the planks of Arby's hideaway shook and parted of their own volition, making a wide gap through which blew the unearthly wind that heralded an attack on Sky. The wind began to howl and blow up again, cascading heaps of dried leaves in through the open entrance into Sky's sanctuary.

In the Land Rover, Arby was trying to avoid the stones in the cutting, but Jane was on his case and wouldn't let up.

'You know what they'll think. That's why I came to find you,' she said. 'That you've run off with the birds. They won't let you do it again.'

Even though she was annoyed with Arby, she still felt protective towards him. She knew how much he enjoyed being involved in the shoot…

Arby was trying to concentrate on his driving, but Sky's frantic voice started bombarding his head.

'Help me! Help me! Help me!' pleaded Sky.

Arby was so distracted that he collided with a huge stone, and both he and Jane were bounced forward by the impact. Arby leapt out of the Land Rover, slammed the door, then scampered back towards the tunnel entrance.

Jane called after him, 'Arby! What is it? Arby!'

Arby paid no heed to her and dived into the tunnel with tremendous urgency, leaving Jane very nonplussed by his behaviour. This was so unlike Arby, she thought. He seemed genuinely frightened of something…

When Arby reached the cavern area where he'd left Sky he got a surprise – Sky was nowhere to be seen. As Arby stared into the empty space where he'd been, he started to wonder if Sky had gone away, just disappeared. He began to hope that he wouldn't return… But then some compulsion made him look up, up to the roof of the tunnel, and he saw that Sky was still with him, and had been pinioned to the tunnel ceiling by tree roots.

All Arby could do was stare in total bewilderment at what he was witnessing. There was nothing he could do to help. He just watched as Sky, with arms flailing, tried to defend himself against the roots, which appeared intent on enveloping him… and then crushing and squeezing the life out of him.

Then, all hell was let loose, and the tunnel was filled with swirling leaves like a swarm of bees. Arby felt totally useless.

Sky still kept calling to him. 'Help me! Help me! Help me!'

Unnerved by the scene, Arby started to make an exit.

'No! No! Please! Please help me! Arby, don't go! Help me!' Sky pleaded with him again.

Arby considered for a few seconds, then made the decision, however hopeless, to do what he could for this strange being that called himself Sky. He moved back shouting, 'How? How?'

With this, the leaves and twigs became a swirling maelstrom. Arby covered his face, then, as suddenly as they'd started, the elements began to calm down. Arby watched as the last fluttering leaves settled on the floor of the tunnel.

Then he saw that Sky was lying prostrate and motionless on the mattress…

Chapter Four
'Dark Satanic Mills'

ARBY LOOKED DOWN AT SKY. He could see no signs of life. There was a sadness in his look – guilt, perhaps, at having been so tardy in coming to Sky's aid? Then suddenly, to Arby's relief, there was a movement.

Sky moved his head a little and addressed Arby in a faltering voice. 'The force against me... I told you... I had... I had to call you... It was tearing me apart...'

'Force? What force?' said Arby.

'The Animus of the Organism.'

Arby was baffled again. 'Who?'

'I told you... It is a mistake, an accident. It is wrong that I am here. I am alien to this time. I must find the Juganet! Do you understand? The Juganet! Then I shall be gone from here! You have witnessed an attempt to reject me as an alien presence… All natural organisms reject that which is foreign to them… or try to… Do you begin to understand?'

Arby thought hard. 'Like, when you're ill, your body tries to fight, reject, the germs?'

At this, Sky began to rise slowly from the mattress, his strength gradually reviving. 'Yes. I… am an intruder. The longer I stay, the stronger the deterrent will become… I will be destroyed… and so will you.'

'Me?' There was a look of disbelief on Arby's face.

Sky nodded. 'Because of the contact between us.'

Sky moved his head to one side. He could see someone hovering a short way behind Arby.

It was Jane, peeking at the proceedings from behind a sheet of metal roofing.

Sky stood up and included her in his warning too. 'Anyone who knows of my existence is in danger of annihilation.'

He raised his arm towards Jane and looked over at her. A blast of light from his eyes and palm turned into a mighty force, which propelled her into the cavern.

Jane steadied herself. 'Oh, Arby, what was that?' She then saw Sky.

'Who are you?' he said sternly.

'That's my sister,' explained Arby.

Jane turned towards Sky and looked him up and down. 'Who does he think he is?'

'You are siblings?' Sky enquired.

Jane went on bravely, 'Who is he, Arby?'

'How much did you hear?' demanded Sky.

Jane was fearful for Arby. Now she could see why he was

being so strange and secretive. He'd got himself involved with some kind of weirdo. She was a bit frightened of his new-found friend, but that was just like Arby – always getting himself into something stupid. Even so, she decided to voice her concern to whoever this very odd person was. 'What are you trying to do to my brother?'

Sky was insistent. 'How much did you hear?'

Jane moved back to stand next to Arby, showing her solidarity. 'Tell me, who is he, Arby?'

'Well… uh…' Arby tried hard to think of a way to explain, but for once, he was literally lost for words. He shrugged, then looked over at Sky and said dismissively. 'You tell her.' Arby thought he'd settled the situation, and saw a good chance to escape. He pulled Jane with him towards the opening. 'Sorry. I've got to go and sort some things out.'

Jane started to go out with him.

'She must stay!' Sky said sharply.

Arby seemed to accept the situation. 'Right then. You hang on then, Jane, I'll…'

Jane crossed him. 'Not leaving me 'ere with 'im are you?'

'Just talk to him. He's alright, he won't hurt you… but don't leave him alone… or he'll be got at, see? Oh, an' his name's Sky.' Arby ducked out through the tunnel.

'Arby, don't be daft! Come back here!' yelled Jane. Then she looked at Sky nervously. Arby had fled, so she had little choice but to accept his wishes.

She turned and took a good long look at her new companion. She found it difficult not to be a wee bit scared, and she wondered if he knew. Jane thought to herself that her brother had dropped her in some pretty strange situations in his time, but this one took the biscuit. Weird.

She was tired of him expecting her to do his dirty work. She only stayed because Arby didn't seem to be afraid of the odd-looking young man.

As she surveyed him, she decided that Sky did look a bit forlorn, lost and pathetic, and the 'wounded animal syndrome' took hold of Jane. Sky didn't look happy, so she decided to try and relax. She was still on alert and still a bit nervous of her charge, but she didn't want to upset him.

Jane walked around the tunnel, whistling to herself to keep her spirits up. She then found a convenient box to sit on, took a *Jackie* magazine from her inside pocket, and settled down to read – all very nonchalant, but aware that Sky had kept her under close observation the whole time. He seemed to be vaguely fascinated by the female of the species, and the way she simply ignored him, but her heart was beating like a drum…

Arby arrived at his home, in the village of Upton Cheyney. It was a pretty village which followed the line of an escarpment overlooking the river Avon.

Arby parked the Land Rover outside his house, a typical small farm labourer's tied cottage. Arby's home was pretty well in its original state – as opposed to the adjacent cottage. It had once been identical to Arby's place, but this was Roy's house, which Major Briggs had 'done up' with little thought of blending in with the existing style. It sported brand new white PVC windows and front door, and a large extension at the side with a conservatory.

Arby leaned into the Land Rover, picked up an empty canvas bag and went into the house. He was intent on taking food to Sky, assuming he was in need of it, but he recalled how he'd rejected the Coke. When he entered the kitchen, there was no sign of anyone around, so he started to fill the canvas bag from the fruit dish.

There was the clack of a metal latch, and Arby's mother came in. She was a warm, kindly soul, with a sort of marshmallow personality. She had no real axe to grind with anyone or anything, and was quite happy to accept her position in society as wife and mother – very unlike her husband's more volatile, slightly leftie, views on how things should be ordered in this life.

Joyce had been conditioned by her parents and upbringing that the world was 'exactly as it should be, and there's an end to it.' Perhaps her only mini-rebellion had been to marry John despite her parents' misgivings about his diametrically opposed political views. True love overcame such detail. She accepted him just as he was, albeit in a resigned sort of way.

What came first for her now was her family, and her children especially. She was so proud of Arby and Jane; they were the focal point of her life. Although it must be said that her almost saintly calm and reserve had been severely tested many times by one or two of her son's antics.

But for now, she was concerned about Arby's absence from the shoot. She saw that Arby looked a bit furtive. He's been up to something, she thought, but decided to let him explain before accusing him.

'Arby. Where you been? They've all been asking for you down at the Barn.'

Arby backed out of the kitchen, keeping the bag out of his mother's sight. 'Just going now mum… Down the Barn. To deliver the pheasants. Bye Mum.'

Arby backed out of the door and was gone.

She tutted, then noticed that he'd taken the fruit from the table. 'Don't have to steal your own stuff, son,' she frowned, and shook her head slowly. 'Funny boy sometimes…'

Jane had made a conscious decision to ignore Sky and continue to appear to be reading her magazine with deep interest.

But Sky was still watching her…

Her eyes shifted to check on Sky now and then. Stop lookin' at me, ya… ya *looker*, she thought angrily. What was he thinking?

She looked up and noticed that Sky was sitting in his lotus position in front of her.

He caught her looking at him and decided it was time to speak. 'You are frightened to – talk?

'Well, what's the point? I don't know what you're on about, that's all. Rabbitin' on. It's all gibberish – this net thing.'

'The Juganet is a circle, which is also a point…'

'Oh yeah?' said Jane sarcastically.

'An intersection of two planes.'

'There you go again! It's no good,' said Jane. There was a steely silence again. Then she had a thought. She couldn't go on trying to make him see sense, so she decided to show an interest. Maybe that might clarify things a bit. 'OK, so this Juganet thing exists, right? So, what's it look like?

'I can only describe it by the forces it generates, not the shape.'

'Oh… so. How'd it get wherever it is?'

'It was put there for the Travellers.'

Jane was struggling to understand. 'Who by?'

'The Others.'

Jane was now beginning to suspect that she was with a complete nutter, and nodded knowingly. Underneath she was frightened to death. 'Others… Oh, I see. Well, uh, how will you know when you find it?'

'I shall be gone, from this place, from this time.'

'Oh, gerroff.' She went back to reading her magazine. I'll certainly be glad when you've gone, thought Jane. Lookin' for a place that don't exist. He's got to be stark, starin' mad.

Arby arrived at the Barn. He took the pheasants out of the back door and was hurrying to deliver them to the shooters when Major Briggs intercepted him.

'What have you been leading my son into?' he demanded, as Arby walked past him. 'You nearly ruined the shoot you know. Keeping us all hanging about like this.' In order to show himself to be in charge of matters concerning the shoot, he shouted orders at Arby for all to hear – telling him to do exactly what he was already doing. 'Now get those birds put up on the table with the rest. That's more like it! Better all be there too, mmm?' he added sharply.

Arby looked back at him with fixed grin.

Briggs turned to the shooters. 'Pick up your birds when you're ready!'

Arby bundled the last few birds into the Land Rover, got into the passenger door and found himself sitting next to his dad.

'Hi, Dad. Alright?' said Arby brightly.

His dad, John Vennor, was in his late forties and had a weather-beaten face beneath short, straight black hair. He nodded toward the back of the Land Rover.

'Got pheasant tonight, have we?' said Vennor, with a sort of complicit grin.

'Don't go there, Dad.'

'What is it then? Where've you been?'

'Just… sort of doin' a favour.'

Mr Vennor flicked his fingers – his sign for Arby to hand over the keys to the vehicle. Arby gave them to him, and he started it.

John Vennor was once a farm worker. He had started as an apprentice in the blacksmith shop just after the war. Within a few short years, all horse-drawn farm implements were being towed by a tractor. He had done some work in an engineering factory and learned to be proficient at welding. He found desultory work repairing tractors and farm equipment. Otherwise he did odd jobs around the village, fence building and anything from painting and decorating to hedging and ditching. He was also the church warden.

John was once a strong socialist. Then with so many changes in farm work – it was all machines now – the union that had protected farm workers had lost its *raison d'etre*. So, our socialist was forced to become self employed. A capitalist! Or as good as, in John Vennor's eyes. However he was quite content with the way things had turned out. In his younger days, John was not beyond doing a bit of poaching from time to time, so he was quite sympathetic and sort of proud (perhaps envious) of Arby's so-called faults. John also had a special dislike of Briggs, who had placed himself above the whole village and reminded John with horror of his National Service days in the army during the 1950s.

He nodded towards the Major. 'Might've lost yourself a job there, boy. Old Briggsy thinks you're trainin' his lad up to be a master criminal.'

Arby forced a smile.

'Where's our Jane? She walkin' back?'

Arby was a bit flummoxed by the question, so not wishing to lie, he grinned and nodded, hiding the real situation as the Land Rover pulled away from the Barn.

Jane was still apparently riveted to her magazine, while Sky was sat in deep trance-like state. He was using his powers to try and understand the history of the people he'd found himself with.

His mind flew though all the points of human life on Earth: Childbirth, evolution, epochs of the past, the early civilisations, Egyptians, Aztecs, Greek, Roman, all forms of art, chemistry, physics, the Renaissance, mathematics, religions, revolutions, the thousands of senseless wars… Sky's mind took on pretty well everything that had shaped the world from its beginning.

He came out of his reverie and addressed Jane. 'This is the first world I have ever seen.'

'There you go again. You must have come from somewhere.'

'I know nothing about this time. I was not briefed or destined for it. I am not ready. I am not yet formed.'

Jane got up and moved around to Sky, slightly bewildered by his sudden childlike, lost-boy sentiment. She was actually quite moved by it, and began to feel concerned for him. 'Sorry, I don't know what you're…' She trailed off, lost for words. Then she decided to come out with her own thoughts on the matter. 'Don't you think people might find you a bit strange? Funny like? All those things you go on about?'

'My journey was interrupted… I do not yet know how to use the powers I have been given.'

'That's daft. What can I say to that? What powers? And what are you?'

'I suppose… in your terms, I am to be a god.'

Jane was stunned into silence by this revelation. It convinced her that he most definitely was quite mad. Quite nice, quite cute even, but quite mad.

Arby's parents were in the kitchen. John Vennor was well into a glass mug of cider. He sipped it, deep in thought.

Mrs Vennor was putting the finishing touches to the pastry edging on a cottage pie with a fork. She looked up at the clock on her way to the oven.

'Look at the time,' she said. 'I hope our Jane don't come back the lane way. It's in a terrible state… all that rain we've had lately.'

Mr Vennor swallowed the last drop of his cider and contemplated the cider barrel on the dresser. He silently debated with himself for a second or two whether he'd have another. He decided he would, he deserved it.

He caught Joyce watching him looking at the barrel, as she put the pie in the oven. 'Bin a hard day love,' he said wearily.

'Always your excuse innit, John Vennor?'

He walked over to the barrel and poured himself another pint.

Mrs Vennor spoke firmly to him. 'Honestly John. You

should've fetched her, but oh no, you'd sooner antagonise him next door.'

'What? Briggs? The gallopin' Major?'

'Respectable people.'

'Him an' his half pints,' said Vennor as he turned the tap off, and held the mug up by the handle to admire the golden liquid in his glass.

'They've only been here a few months and you've done nothing but antagonise him. I don't know what young Roy must think.'

Vennor grinned knowingly. 'Got his eye on our Jane, hasn' he?'

'If you say so. Well, where is she anyway?'

Mr Vennor took his drink back to his chair and jumped, as the door flew open and Arby rushed into the kitchen. He put his canvas bag down.

'Where's your sister?' asked Joyce.

'Just goin' for her now, Mum,' replied Arby, trying not to look his mother in the eye. He moved past her to his dad. 'Can I have the keys again, Dad?'

'Again? In me jacket.' He nodded to it hanging behind the door.

Arby fished in the jacket pocket for the keys.

'Don't hang about this time,' his dad warned.

Mrs Vennor tried to take a look into the canvas bag that Arby had put down. 'Here? What's that?' she said, still wondering what was in it.

Arby snatched it from her before she could identify what it was. 'Just goin' to get Jane. Cheers. See you later.'

Arby swept out.

Mrs Vennor folded her arms and shook her head in mock

despair. She knew there was something afoot and would really like to know what. Arby was being evasive, a sure sign he was up to no good.

'That lad of ours is up to something – an' he's got our Jane in on it with him, I'll bet.'

'Right pair.' Vennor smiled at the thought of his children being disruptive and continued to sip his cider.

Major Briggs was standing in his sparsely-furnished lounge, staring into the distance, recalling the days when he was in Tripoli. Cushy number that, he thought. Then came visions of cool evenings on the terrace drinking gin... of soldierly comradeship and the idiotic tomfoolery that he and his brother officers got up to... What fantastic days they were!

A smile crossed his lips. Still with a thoughtful and faraway look in his eye, the Major poured himself a drink from a litre jug of ready-mixed gin and tonic with ice and lemon slices. He tasted the drink, and murmured his satisfaction. It was the perfect reward for him, after fielding the somewhat messy events of the day, which were still troubling him. Briggs was very concerned that the village people should respect him, even if they didn't like him. His conviction was that his rank and standing were very precious to him and should be understood. Yes, he thought, he should be looked up to by the neighbourhood, and why not? He found it hard to understand why the villagers – those below the rank of the vicar, and the people on the old Grange, and perhaps the pub landlord, or perhaps not – didn't understand that officers, who have spent their life in the service of the monarch, deserved a certain amount of respect.

By then, the gin had begun to take the edge off the day's problems and help him take on a warm glow. He continued his reverie about better days in the army, where everything was clear – who you were and all that. You gave orders to those below you and obeyed orders from those above you. Simple, straightforward…

His reflective mood was shattered by the noise of Roy clattering down the stairs. The boy came into the lounge with a crash helmet in hand. The Major looked at him askance, and jumped to the immediate conclusion that he was off to join the oiks next door.

'Look, lad, I don't want the police round here. Keep away from those two next door, d'you understand?'

Roy gave a flat, 'OK, Dad,' and just walked straight past him.

The Major shouted at him impotently as the front door slammed shut. 'Just you watch it laddie! Or I'll…' then muttered softly into the empty space, 'Right.'

He was hopeless as a parent and knew it, but he'd decided to try and maintain a simple code of conduct with his son. One of respect for each other. It had started reasonably well, but the boy was constantly eroding it. These days, Roy seemed moody and recalcitrant, even rude at times. The Major had no real idea how to assert himself and bring his authority to bear. Most probably it was because he felt guilty about leaving the boy to be brought up by his mother and being absent from his life for so long…

These thoughts flashed through his mind before he decided to make a positive move. After all, he was only thinking of protecting Roy…

He took another gulp of his drink, rolled his shoulders

and said decisively, 'Right my lad.' He then marched out after Roy.

Arby had joined Jane and Sky in the tunnel. He took the canvas bag off his shoulder, took out some fruit and biscuits, and offered them to Sky.

'Thought you must be hungry? Well here's some food for you.'

Sky frowned. 'I do not know how to eat.'

Arby proffered a packet of biscuits and tore the seal open for him. 'Well you can practice on these biscuits.'

Sky made no move to take them. 'I do not need to eat…'

'I do,' said Jane, as she took the biscuits from him.

'They're for 'im!' insisted Arby.

'He don't want 'em does he?'

Arby ignored her and turned to his bag. He threw some clothes over to Sky, a T-shirt and a pair of trousers. 'Here's some gear for you.'

'Gear?' Sky fingered the texture of the trousers.

'Clothes,' said Arby, tugging at his shirt and jumper to explain. 'To wear? I mean, if we're goin' lookin' for this Juganet thing, you can't go round in your birthday suit, can you?'

It was Sky's turn to be nonplussed.

It was dark outside now. Arby, with Jane in the passenger seat next to him, drove through the cutting with headlights full on…

Behind them, in the back of the Land Rover, sat Sky. He was now wearing the clothes that Arby had brought for him.

Roy, riding his motorbike, intercepted them, but Arby was so intent on driving his new acquaintance to safety that he failed to see Roy waving at them.

Roy was confused by Arby's action. He turned his bike around and went off after them.

Completely unnoticed by Arby or Jane, a howling wind bent the trees the Land Rover passed towards them. Showers of loose leaves kicked up behind the speeding vehicle and swirled into mini twisters as a reaction to Sky's presence…

Sky noticed the tumult directed at him, but knew it was pointless to show his concern and turned to Arby. 'You travel in strange directions?'

'All like that 'round here. Lanes and that. I'm takin' you to a place of learning. Might be able to track down that thing you're lookin' for.'

'The Juganet?'

Jane suddenly realised something. 'Nobody there this time of night. You'll have to break in, Arby.'

Sky frowned, concerned. 'Why? How is this knowledge stored?'

Roy lost the Land Rover. He tried a different road, but circled back again. He then decided to take the main road. The Bath to Bristol, on what's called the 'upper road', took him past the local school on the western outskirts of Bath.

As he passed the building, he just happened to catch sight of the Land Rover parked outside the sign that read Merriam Comprehensive School.

It was a modern building, all glass and concrete, and was the school that he and Jane still attended – and that Arby had recently left with rather bad results.

Roy circled around and parked his bike in the shadows, then went off to look for Arby and Jane. He noticed that the school gate was wide open, went through and kept to the shadows.

Jane had been posted as a lookout at the corner of the building. Arby and Sky were at the glazed front entrance door. She was getting a bit jittery. After all, this was breaking and entering. It wasn't stuff that 'fell off a lorry.' This, apart from everything else, was a real actual crime that her brother was getting her involved with.

She called to Arby in a loud whisper. 'Hurry up, Arby!'

Arby was trying desperately to get the school entrance door open, pushing and pulling at the lock to no avail.

'I am! Can't you see?' he replied angrily.

Sky was watching Arby from behind and asked him patiently, 'What are you trying to do?'

'Open it.'

'Let me,' said Sky.

'How?'

Sky focused his strange blue eyes on the door lock, which began to flash in different translucent colours, accompanied by a staccato, high-pitched piercing noise…

Silence. And then the doors flew open.

'Is that not alright?' asked Sky.

Arby was speechless for a second, but he quickly pulled himself together and started into the school. Jane went to follow him, but he held her arm to stop her. 'You stay here an' keep an eye out, OK?'

Jane obeyed him with a nod and carried on keeping a look out while Arby entered the school with Sky. Jane was full of concern for the danger she'd been put in, all because of the weirdo that Arby had decided to befriend. What will it all come to? she thought, quoting a lament her mother often used.

Inside the school, Arby crept around the darkened corridors, trying doors, hoping to find an open one. At last he found a classroom with an unlocked door and Sky followed him in.

Jane was suddenly petrified when a huge shadow that resembled a spaceman appeared on the wall… She then realised with relief that it was cast by Roy in his 'bone dome' crash helmet, and relaxed as he approached her.

'What the hell are you doing here?' he said.

Jane shushed him.

'Who was that with you and Arby?'

'Nobody,' Jane insisted.

'OK… Leave you to it then shall I?' Roy turned to walk away.

They were alerted by the sound of a car driving up to the school.

'Look out, somebody's coming!' warned Jane. She pushed Roy through the school doors, and they ran into the dark corridors.

The new arrival at the school gates was Major Briggs. He had recognised Roy's motorbike parked by the school. Then, when he saw the Land Rover, he decided that the Vennors were up to no good as usual – and that Roy was in danger of becoming involved. He took a torch from the glove compartment, got out, walked in through the open gate and cautiously approached the school to investigate.

In the classroom, Arby had piled loads of books in front of Sky, who was sitting at one of the desks.

Sky flicked through each one, obviously not reading the words, but seeming to be avidly digesting the contents.

Arby dumped another pile of books beside him. 'Any good?'

'This is a laborious way to store information,' Sky stated simply. He flicked through another book.

Arby watched him in growing annoyance. I've broken into the damn school for him an' his Juganet, he thought.

'So why don't you read 'em?' he asked.

'I have,' said Sky.

Arby made a face; he'd been put down again.

Then Sky picked on a picture in an astronomy book, a picture of a radio telescope. He suddenly seemed interested. 'Where is this?'

Arby looked at the picture. 'Australia.'

'Is that near here?'

'No. Not really.'

Sky flicked over a few more pages and stopped again, this time at a double page cutaway picture of the CERN cyclotron. 'And this? What is this called?'

'That's the cyclotron, for smashin' atoms.'

Sky looked up from the book. He was sensing something… He suddenly stood up. 'Someone is approaching.'

'Jane?'

'No… not Jane.'

Outside the class window, a tree was flailing around in

a strong wind. It hit the window with a crack. Sky became concerned…

The Major was searching the dark school corridor, with the torch. He called out softly but with some urgency. 'Roy?'

Roy was hiding behind a cupboard in the shadows with Jane.

The Major missed them and shuffled past.

'Roy?' He turned around another corridor. By now, the Major was getting a bit annoyed so he decided to use a more commanding tone. 'Hello there? Come on out. Come on!' He saw a dim light coming from a classroom and approached it cautiously. 'Who's there? Who is it? Is that you, Vennor?'

There was a flash of energy from the darkness. It had issued from Sky's outstretched open palm. The Major was stopped in his tracks. He let the torch drop to the floor, then crashed to the floor himself and lay there unconscious and rigid, as if frozen…

Arby rushed over to the Major to see if he was alright.

The Major opened his eyes, blinked and tried to focus on Arby who was kneeling next to him. Sky was behind him, standing in the middle of the corridor, looking down at them with that pitiless stare of his.

'Sky. What did you do?' asked a very worried Arby.

'I don't know. Who is he? I thought it was – something else.' Sky kept his own council, but thought that his enemy had now been made manifest.

'It's Roy's dad.'

Arby looked down at the Major's staring eyes. 'What's the matter with him? What have you done to him?'

They heard clattering footsteps from along the corridor and Roy appeared around the corner. He took in the scene and looked hard at Arby.

'It's your dad, Roy…' Arby said.

Roy went over to his dad and cradled his head. 'Dad, you alright?'

The Major gasped and stared up at Roy.

'Dad!'

The Major groaned and nodded his head toward Sky.

Then Roy saw Sky for the first time and glared at him angrily. 'You did this.'

Jane then stumbled in on the scene. 'What happened?'

'He will recover,' said Sky, doing his best to try and placate Roy in some way.

'He can't move. He's paralysed!'

'It is not a permanent condition.'

Sky stared at Arby. 'Arby… we have not finished.' He was willing Arby to obey and return to the classroom.

Arby obediently moved back to the classroom.

Jane knelt down with Roy to tend to his father.

'How in God's name did you get mixed up with him?' said Roy irritably.

Jane had no idea how to explain what had happened and decided to change the subject. 'We ought to get your dad to a doctor.'

The Major groaned again and seemed to recover a little.

'Come on, sit him up,' said Jane.

She and Roy helped Major Briggs up to a sitting position.

In the classroom, Sky was studying an atlas of Britain.

Arby pointed out their position on the map. 'We're about here.'

'Are these the lines of force?' said Sky, as he ran his finger over the grid lines.

'No. That's just the grid,' replied Arby.

Sky looked at the window, where the wind-blown tree was flailing at the panes of glass. He stood up with some urgency. 'We must go.' He started to move, the atlas still in his hand.

Arby stopped him. 'You can't take that. It belongs –'

'Is not this knowledge available to all?'

Arby wasn't happy, but didn't back down. He took the book from Sky, then went to the door.

Outside, in the corridor, Roy managed to steady his father as he stood up shakily. Then Roy and Jane helped him to walk falteringly along the corridor.

'Come on, Dad, let's get you home,' said Roy as they steered him to the door.

The Major turned back to see Sky and Arby outside the classroom. 'You're not getting away with this, understand?'

Roy was about to put his oar in, but the Major pulled him away. 'No, lad, don't say anything. The less said the better. We'll get this sorted out, don't you worry.' Then he added, loaded with the threat of possible legal procedures to come, 'You'll be hearing from us… Alright?'

Roy held on to his father's arm as they moved off towards the school doors.

Jane turned to Sky and Arby exasperated and close to tears. 'That's it then. He's bound to tell the police. We'll all get put in the slammer!' Then she looked directly at Sky. 'Why d'you hit him?'

'He didn't hit him,' argued Arby.

'Well he did something,' said Jane.

Sky spoke up, adamant. 'Your little problems do not concern me. I must find the Juganet. Or...'

'Or what?' said Jane.

'The force against me is becoming manifest...' said Sky with deep concern.

In the Vennor's kitchen, Mr and Mrs Vennor looked on as the Major poured himself a large whisky from the quarter bottle they kept for medicinal, or special, occasions.

The amount poured was not missed by Mr Vennor. Oh, go on, take the lot why don't you? he thought. That's not for drinkin...

But in the circumstances and as the host, he would seem mean if he didn't accept it.

'No sooner saw him when... Bang! I was out cold. Must have used an iron rod or something,' said Briggs, contemplating his whiskey.

'And they're still with this feller?' asked Mr Vennor.

But Briggs was too concerned about his injuries and the total injustice of it all to answer the question. 'Completely paralysed me... couldn't move.' Then he included Roy. 'He was there, weren't you, eh lad?'

Mrs Vennor turned to Roy. 'What were they doin' down there Roy?'

The Major answered before Roy could speak. 'Oh, they'd broken in hadn't they?'

'What?' said Mrs Vennor. She began to see the seriousness

of the situation, and was very keen to get some answers, but she let the Major plough on.

'Oh, no, no, no, not your two, they just tagged along… no. It was the… other one, the older one. Vicious little swine. I reckon he'd run off from somewhere y'know.'

Mr Vennor was now very concerned, and went for his coat on the back of the door. 'We'll soon find out. Use your vehicle can we, sir?'

Roy and the Major got up, ready to leave with him.

Mr Vennor opened the door for them, but before he left, he popped his head back around the door to Joyce and said, 'And… love, I think you'd better get on to Joe Simmonds.'

Jane and Arby came out of the school, and hurried off to the Land Rover. Jane was still deeply concerned about the events she'd witnessed.

When Sky came through the door after them, he was immediately attacked by swirling leaves and twigs. The strange gale had got up again.

Sky sounded really frightened when he called, 'Arby!'

On hearing his desperate cries, even Jane decided they have to help him. 'Come on, Arby. Sky's in trouble, we've gotta help him.'

'Changed your tune haven't you? Come on then!'

They ran back to get him, but when they reached the school entrance, Sky had disappeared… there was just a heap of twigs and leaves.

Arby had a quick look around, but then came Sky's cries again.

'Arby! Help me!' The cries were coming from the woods next to the school.

Arby rushed off into the woods, to search for him. 'Sky! Where are you? Sky!'

It was at that moment that Mr Vennor, Major Briggs and Roy arrived at the school in the Major's car. After getting out, they heard Arby's shouts from the woods.

Roy called back to him, 'Arby!' and ran off towards the sound of his voice.

As Briggs followed after his son, Mr Vennor became aware of the strange howling wind approaching them… He was fascinated at first but then felt a little unnerved by it.

'Bit of a freaker… this wind,' he said.

'What?' said the Major, as he turned to him.

'No wind back on the road.'

They plodded on after the kids.

In the wooded area close by, the stump of a tree trunk was bathed in an eerie greenish light… The wind whipped around it, and soon became a ferocious whirlwind… In the middle of the tree stump, something began to emerge… It was at first like swirling black smoke, which then became solid and took on a form reminiscent of a bat. It grew and changed, then the dark shape seemed to dance in the wind vortex… It then gradually assumed the shape of a black cloak… The cloak was on the shoulders of a man… This figure, a tall, grey haired, bearded man slowly raised his head.

This creature was formed from the metamorphosis of living organic matter into the form of a man, created by nature itself, with one specific purpose: to destroy the alien presence on the Earth, Sky. He was called Goodchild…

*

Sky staggered alone through the wood, then stopped. He could sense danger was close by. He was not far from where the sinister black-cloaked figure had appeared…

From the crest of a sloping hill, Goodchild looked down at Sky and waved his arms, summoning nature to do its work and annihilate this abomination…

Sky fell to the ground and the natural elements around him again began to cover him. He made a great effort to sit up and face the figure that that was now approaching him. He raised his palm and was about to use the force he had within him against his enemy… when Arby arrived, tumbling down from a ridge.

Arby pushed Sky's arm down. 'No, Sky!'

Then he too looked up – at what appeared to be an ugly, gnome-like, bearded face…

Chapter Five
'Goodchild'

ARBY AND SKY FOUND THEMSELVES looking up at the bulky, bearded frame of Police Sergeant Simmonds, who was wearing his poncho-type rain cape…

Some time later, at the police station, Mr and Mrs Vennor, Major Briggs, Roy, Jane, Arby and Sky were waiting anxiously to hear what Sergeant Simmonds, who was holding the telephone to his ear, would say, when he spoke to the constabulary records office.

He half grinned at the assembly before him, and stroked his straggly beard as he waited. 'Ah, Simmonds here… Stanton Gurney… Collator please. Hello… yeah. We got a lad here, could be a runaway… Saying nothin' as usual…' He looked

Sky up and down then continued. 'Late teens I'd say – five ten, slim build, collar length fair hair, pale complexion and – ah, blue eyes.' He listened. 'Well, breakin' and enterin' and assault so far. He's dumped his own clothes.'

Simmonds turned to Arby. 'That right Arby?'

Arby just shrugged in answer.

'Could you check hostels, corrective centres, remand, the lot? Oh, I'd say he'd been on the run since last night. That right, son?'

Sky stared back at Simmonds in silence.

'No, he still won't say anythin'. Cheers then… thanks.' Sergeant Simmonds stood up from his desk. 'Right, well, if you wouldn't mind, ah, I need a bit of a chat with the lad here, find out what's what.' He indicated for them to leave him with Sky. 'I'll have to get a statement from the lad. I'm sure you understand I need to talk to him alone.' He ushered them out of his office.

The Major turned and insisted on making his case. 'Well, Sergeant, I think you ought to know –'

Simmonds cut him off firmly. 'I'll take your statement later, Mr Briggs.'

'Oh yes, of course, of course. You carry on.' And he followed the others out the office and closed the door.

Simmonds grinned at Sky and went to his chair, confident he could deal with this young whipper-snapper.

The sergeant was one of a veritable breed of country copper, slightly overweight, but bicycle borne, and for the most part, on the face of it, apparently jolly. The last thing Simmonds wanted in this job was trouble. He relied on local knowledge, and knowing enough about country matters, to be trusted by the people in the community. He'd learned to take it easy on, or turn a blind eye to, things that didn't seem too important, and even overlooked some lesser incursions of the law – poaching for instance… But he went in hard when he was sure a real crime, such as theft and violence against the person, had taken place. He was at ease with most of the people on his beat and in turn, he was generally treated with respect.

Simmonds looked Sky over. He'd met his type before he thought, and in fact he felt a bit sorry for this waif. He also felt perfectly sure that he knew exactly how to deal with him. Simmonds was not at all the aggressive type and believed in the softly-softly approach. So, his manner was that of a slightly weary, but friendly, older relation. A 'sorry, but this is my job. It's a real pain for me, but it's got to be done' sort of attitude.

'Right then, son, sit down. Sky? That some sort of nickname is it?'

Sky simply stood and stared at Simmonds, who was trying to be as matter-of-fact as he could.

'Oh come on now. There's nothin' to be afraid of.'

'Why should I be afraid?' said Sky.

'What were you after? Down at the school… Eh?'

Sky remained utterly inscrutable.

Simmonds reiterated his question. 'What were you after?'

Sky considered, then answered. 'Knowledge.'

Simmonds lost his grin, frowned and wondered what Sky's game was. The lad was beginning to sound a wee bit cheeky, and Sergeant Simmonds decided he would have none of that. 'Watch it son, don't try an' get clever with me,' he warned. Then to ease things up again, he gave a wide smile, and tried another tack. 'Now, there's no need to make it hard on yourself. Few simple questions, that's all. Now then. What's your full name? Where d'you come from and what're you doin' here? That's all we want to know.'

Sky stared hard again at the sergeant, then said assertively, 'It does not concern you what my name is, or where I have come from, or where I am going.' Sky pressed his words home as he concentrated a withering stare into the sergeant's eyes. Sky was using his powers in order to avoid any further trouble from what he considered as utterly irrelevant people.

Simmonds quickly became mesmerised by Sky's steady stare. He had been put into a sort of trance. He was silent and frozen to the spot for a short while. Then, when he came out of it, he continued speaking – for all the world as if Sky had filled him in with all the information he needed. He smiled warmly at Sky and went on in a bright, satisfied tone. 'Now that's more like it son. Didn't hurt, did it? Bit of co-operation, that's all we need.'

He picked up the telephone and dialled a number. 'Simmonds again. You can forget about that ID on the lad, it's all been sorted out… I can deal with it… Assault? No. All blown up from nothing… Yes, I can deal with him here. Cheers then.' Simmonds got up and opened the door and called, 'Mr Briggs?'

Briggs responded and entered the office. As he passed Simmonds, he muttered, sotto voice, almost swallowing the words, 'It's ah… Major… yes, Major Briggs. Right, er, Sergeant?' He hated always having to remind people of his rank, which was still valid for life even though he'd retired.

As a police officer, Simmonds should know that. Briggs suspected that he did but that, like some of the people in the rest of the village, he liked to antagonise the Major.

The sergeant turned and faced Briggs. 'Now, you claim the young man here assaulted you?'

'Yes. Definitely.'

'With a weapon of some kind?'

'It felt like a damn great iron bar,' said the Major, touching the spot on his head gingerly.

Simmonds scrutinised the Major, then began to move around to the back of his head to take a good look at it. He tried to find a wound of some sort, but could see nothing.

'Whereabouts did he hit you, Mr Briggs?'

Briggs became nervous and defensive under Simmonds' sceptical gaze.

Simmonds took a closer look, then shook his head. He was absolutely certain there was no wound at all to be seen. 'Iron bar'd make a pretty nasty wound, eh? Nothin' there that I can see Mr Briggs. Not even a swellin' or anything.'

At home, the Major was pouring himself another drink. He was still mystified by the whole situation. Roy was sitting on the sofa with an open motorcycle magazine, but he wasn't reading it. There was a bit of an atmosphere and Roy was using his magazine to keep himself out of things.

Then his father started to mumble. 'Must have been a stick… or something…'

Roy remonstrated with his father, obviously from an on-going disagreement. 'Look, Dad, he must have hit you with something. Couldn't you see?'

Briggs remained pensive as he sipped his drink.

'Completely unprovoked,' he said miserably, as he stalked off. 'I'm damn well going to ring my solicitor.'

'Yes. I should, Dad.' Roy put his nose back into the magazine, but then had an idea. He decided to go out instead.

Briggs turned to him as he was dialling. 'Where are you off to?'

'Oh, I'm just going to put the bike away,' said Roy.

He went through the kitchen, then Briggs popped his head through the serving hatch and warned. 'Stay away from next door.'

'OK,' said Roy sharply.

'At least until that hooligan's out of the way. Why they agreed to take him in I'll never know...'

A tall figure in a black cloak moved slowly along the forest track. It was Goodchild, the personification of nature's power. His raven-like eyes were scanning the tree-line that fringed the road.

He headed purposefully toward it...

Sky had been allowed to leave the police station and was now in the back of the Land Rover, travelling with the Vennor family.

Joyce, always determined to be welcoming and polite, turned to Sky. 'Just till tomorrow, is it?' she said.

'I must go,' insisted Sky.

'Oh, no, it's not that it's any trouble or anything, honestly.' Joyce was her ebullient self, but secretly felt a bit wary of Arby's new-found friend. He seemed rootless and she felt there was something sad about him. But her mouth said,

'You're welcome to stay as long as you like. That's right isn't it, John?'

Mr Vennor nodded and grinned. He was secretly delighted and highly amused by the way things had turned out – with maximum discomfiture to the hoity-toity Major Briggs, who was always hinting about how he was different, more refined, than them. 'And if the gallopin' Major don't like it he knows what he can do,' Mr Vennor couldn't resist saying.

At the school, Roy turned the corner of the corridor where his father had been knocked out. The torch was on the floor, along with the atlas Arby had carried for Sky. Roy picked them up, then decided to look into the classroom where Sky had been. He saw the pile of books that he'd been looking at. Roy then felt a presence in the room with him. His hair stood on end as he heard the sound of a howling wind in the classroom…

He turned slowly to see the frightening visage of Goodchild glowering down at him, eyes like gimlets.

'I'm looking for my charge…' said Goodchild.

Roy, relying on the adrenalin of fear, made a dash for it out of the classroom.

Goodchild watched him go. Smiling contemptuously, he then became like a vapour and disappeared.

The Land Rover was winding its way back along the road to the house. Without warning, the vehicle came upon the sinister black clad figure of Goodchild standing in the middle of the road.

Vennor swerved to avoid him.

Goodchild then disappeared as quickly as he'd come.

The Land Rover careered off into the hedge and ended up crashing into a stone wall. The impact caused the door to fly open and Mrs Vennor was thrown out. She landed on the ground by the front wheel and hit her head on a wooden post.

Vennor and the kids rushed to her. She appeared to be unconscious.

'Joyce! Joyce!' shouted Vennor.

Sky stood behind, watching as they tended to Mrs Vennor.

They gently rolled her over and Vennor looked anxiously down the road. 'Where's that bloke? I must have hit him! You saw him, didn't you Arby? You must have seen him.'

'Dad it's alright. He's not here, is he?'

'Dad, her breathing's gone all funny!' yelled Jane.

'What are we gonna do?' said Vennor. 'If I could get my hands in that bloke I'd –'

Sky stared down at the group. 'Concussion. You must get her home.'

'You're not supposed to move 'em… are you?' said Jane.

'You must get her home.' Sky was adamant.

At the Briggs's house, the Major was deep in thought as he looked at the plans of a plastic model Centurion tank he was building. He was disturbed by a loud rapping at the door and got up to see who it was. He opened his door to be confronted by a very worried looking Vennor.

'There's been an accident!'

'Not Roy?'

'No. It's Joyce. Can I use your phone to get the doctor?'

'Yes, of course, go ahead.' Briggs followed Vennor into the lounge. 'Is she badly hurt?'

'She hurt her head… out cold.'

'Oh dear, I'm sorry.'

Vennor dialed the doctor. 'Some damn fool stepped right out in front of us… Doctor Marshall? John Vennor here, Upton Cheyney. It's the wife.'

A while later, Doctor Marshall, the Vennor's GP, was ushered in to their lounge by John.

Jane and Arby were drinking cups of tea. Arby was still confused by the accident and he confided in Jane.

'It's weird. Dad must have hit that bloke. He *must* have! He didn't stand a chance.'

'Where was he though? Why couldn't we find him?' said Jane. She looked over at Sky, standing by the door. Her eyes narrowed. 'You know don't you?' She went up to Sky and challenged him. 'Well?'

'It was not a man you saw.'

'What d'you mean?' said Arby.

'I told you he knew.'

'It is the force against me, made manifest.'

'Why our mum? She didn't do anything,' said Jane.

'You are all in danger.'

The kitchen door opened and Vennor entered, followed by the doctor.

'How is she, Dad?' said Arby.

'Doctor says she should have come round by now.'

'I had your father call an ambulance,' said the doctor.

'Shouldn't be long,' said Vennor. He tried hard to keep up a confident smile, but he was genuinely concerned.

'Couple of x-rays and we'll be able see what's what,' said the doctor.

Roy got back home. He went into the living room, to find his father fiddling with his model tank.

'Is that the doctor's car next door?' asked Roy.

'Yes, there's been an accident. Mrs Vennor… could have been you, you know. Where have you been?'

'The school.'

'The what?'

'Well, you said he hit you with something. So I went and –'

'I told you to keep out of this,' snapped his father.

'I'm only trying to help.'

'Well don't…' Then, as Roy moved away. 'Did you… ah… find anything?'

'No, not really.' Roy moved off to his bedroom.

Briggs watched him go… then went back to working on his model.

Vennor was pacing up and down the kitchen. The situation was causing a bit of tension which expressed itself as a rather pointless argument between Arby and his dad.

'Ambulance should be here by now.'

'Takes a good twenty minutes, Dad,' said Arby.

'Not if you come round the bypass.'

'Takes just as long on a Saturday.'

'Not if you cut up through Clay Hill.'

'You can't, 'cause it's one way now.'

'Oh don't argue all the time!'

Jane came between them. 'Dad! For goodness sake!'

Sky took note of the rising tension and slipped, unseen, out of the room and into the lounge.

In the Vennor's lounge, Sky moved in and stood over Joyce Vennor's prostrate body. She was lying on the couch, still in a deep coma. Sky was concerned that if he intervened in any way he would be using up vital energy that would be needed for the conflict to come…

Then, he made his choice and stared down at her. As he did so, his eyes began to change colour into glaring red, orange and green, and then to pitch black… Again they became windows into the cosmos. Stars and galaxies appeared to be inside and behind them. Sky then raised his hands and stretched them out in front of him… The palms of his hands followed suit and brilliant colours changed until they also turned into black space with the stars and galaxies appearing in them… He moved close to Mrs Vennor. His hands and eyes then slowly scanned over her body.

In the kitchen, Vennor, was still very het-up as he checked his watch yet again.

'More than twenny minutes now.'

Jane served a sandwich to Arby and said. 'It'll get here when it gets here, Dad. Don't worry.'

The lounge door opened slowly and, to everyone's total amazement, Mrs Vennor came into the kitchen, frizzing her hair and yawning as if she'd just woken up from a nap. She suddenly noticed that the assembly in the kitchen was all looking at her in complete and utter surprise. She became a bit embarrassed, as if there was something wrong with her dress or hair.

'What you all…?' she said.

'Joyce!' said Vennor, eyes wide with surprise and relief.

Joyce looked at the doctor quizzically. 'Doctor Marshall? What you doin' here?'

The doctor rose and approached her, trying to assess her medical condition. He held her wrist to take her pulse, and then put his forefinger in front of her eyes and said, 'Mrs Vennor, follow my finger with your eyes, please.'

He moved his raised forefinger from left to right, and then back again. He then moved his finger towards her forehead, checking her eye reaction for depth and balance.

Joyce played along with the doctor's tests, but was highly embarrassed at the same time.

Doctor Marshall then held both her hands in his as he looked at her pupils.

Joyce became concerned.

The doctor let go of her hands with a shrug. 'Well she seems alright. I can't tell for sure,' he said.

'There's really no need to have got you out… is there?'

'No trouble at all, Mrs Vennor. But it's best to be sure, you know. Now you come and sit down,' said the doctor, in a calming voice.

John rushed over to take hold of her, but the doctor restrained him with a raised hand.

'Don't worry, and don't say anything,' said the doctor, giving Vennor a cautioning look.

Arby offered the doctor the chair next to his mum.

Doctor Marshall sat down and took charge. 'Now, Mrs Vennor, do you remember the accident?'

She looked at him askance, then thought things over and recalled, 'Well I remember us swerving and me grabbing the door.' She looked at the staring faces all around her, worried. 'What you all staring at me like that for?'

The replies were silenced by the sound of an ambulance siren outside the house.

'There's the ambulance.' Vennor hurried out to greet it.

Joyce her brow furrowed with concern. 'What? Ambulance? Whatever for? Look, this is silly.'

The doctor touched her hand sympathetically, and insisted. 'I think I'd like you to have a few x-rays, just to be on the safe side.'

'What for?' exclaimed Joyce.

'Nothing to be worried about, just making sure. Belt and braces, eh, Mrs Vennor? Funny thing, concussion.'

John confided to her. 'You was out cold, love.'

The doctor patted her shoulder. 'Now, come along.'

John gently helped her up from the chair. She moved unwillingly towards the door, protesting at the thought of hospital and all that went with it. 'But I haven't had a wash and the kids – they haven't had their teas and we got a guest, that friend of yours, Arby.'

She was bundled out to the waiting ambulance. Arby and Jane watched her go.

Their Dad turned back to them. 'You two hold the fort while we're gone. Look after your friend.'

'OK Dad,' said Arby and he closed the door behind him. He looked around the kitchen and called. 'Sky? Where is he?' But he was nowhere to be seen.

Arby opened the lounge door and looked in. He saw Sky lying on the couch just as Joyce had been. He too was apparently unconscious. Arby rushed up to him. He noticed that he was breathing, but with some difficulty.

Sky managed to speak in a frail, strained voice. 'Rest... I must rest now.'

Arby turned to Jane who was at the door. 'Come on, give me a hand. Come on – let's get him up to the spare room.'

Arby and Jane carried Sky up the stairs and into their spare room, where they laid him on a bare mattress.

Jane rubbed her arms. 'Cold in 'ere.'

'Put that sleeping bag over him.' Arby pointed to a rolled up sleeping bag.

Sky addressed Arby. He sounded desperate. 'Stay... you must stay with me. It is important that you stay with me.'

They rolled the bag out on top of him and Jane tucked it in.

'There, you'll be alright, you're safe in here and we're just downstairs,' said Jane.

Sky tried to talk, but seemed to be swimming in and out of consciousness. 'The force... I... the... force.' He closed his eyes. Sky desperately needed time to re-gather his strength. He knew he would have to face Goodchild again soon. Since his untimely landing, the powers that had been given to him were immature and still going through a kind of re-booting – a sort of plan 'B' to compensate for his inaccurate arrival time.

During his rest time, the unique axons, synapses and neural pathways in Sky's brain were gradually re-assembling themselves to enable him to build enough strength to reflect cosmic energy. The problem was that he needed time to allow this to happen, not only to combat Goodchild, but also to carry out his future mission. He knew that time was of the essence, but the more he used his powers on less important things, the weaker he would become… and therefore, laid open to destruction…

A hand went to the knocker of the Briggs's house and rapped hard, three times. Bang. Bang. Bang.

Roy opened the door, but before he could react, the sinister figure of Goodchild, now dressed in a smart suit and tie, pushed brusquely past him and on into the house.

'Your father, boy,' he commanded.

In the kitchen, the Major was in the middle of cooking supper. He was wearing an apron. He sauntered into the lounge to see who the caller was. On seeing the visitor, the Major took the apron off quickly and bundled it behind a cushion on a chair. He looked up and stared at Goodchild, racking his brain, trying desperately to figure out who this man was.

'I have disturbed you… James,' said Goodchild.

On hearing his Christian name used, the Major was even more confused, his eyes narrowed trying hard to remember him, but still couldn't figure out who he was.

'James… Jimmy?' boomed Goodchild. 'Don't you remember? Ambrose? Captain Ambrose Goodchild.'

Briggs puzzled over the name and then seemed to recollect something. He looked worried and spluttered out. 'Ambrose… yes. But-but-but they told me you were… they told me that you were… uh…'

'Did they? Me?'

'Of course, I didn't believe them. What?' He began to chuckle at the idea. 'Old Ambrose dead?'

'What did you say about it?' said Goodchild.

'Oh, how long ago is it now?' Still confused, the Major

sought a crutch to steady him. He moved over to his drinks table. 'Drink? G'n'T, wasn't it? Your tipple? Right?' He poured two glasses. Then nodded at Roy, with the inference that he wanted him to clear off.

Roy took the hint and left. 'I'll go to my bedroom and read.' He moved away up the stairs.

'Well, Ambrose, eh?' Briggs handed Goodchild a drink. 'Oh, well... yes, well.' He raised his glass with a flat smile. 'Cheers.'

Goodchild smiled back at him evilly. 'Chin, chin.'

Briggs took a slurp, then, still mystified, battled on. 'Well... Old Ambrose, eh? What brings you round these parts then?

'An investigation... Jimmy.'

'Oh?' The Major was suddenly interested and gave him an encouraging nod.

Then Goodchild's voice boomed out. 'The law has been broken.'

He had now harnessed the Major in his power.

The Major began to stare blankly into Goodchild's mesmeric eyes.

Goodchild continued his homily. 'There is an intruder. He must be dealt with.' He then stepped back, leaving the Major frozen, like a statue, gazing into space.

Goodchild moved slowly out of the room into the hallway. As he began to mount the stairs, he became a blur. When he re-appeared, his clothes had changed, reverting to the long black cloak...

Next door, Jane was sitting on the stairs, going over events with Arby.

'Our mum could have got killed tonight. Look Arby, it's all been plonked on us hasn't it? Suppose we tell 'em. We should you know.'

Arby mumbled what sounded like agreement, then he nodded. He'd decided. 'Alright, we do. We tell 'em… It's not as if we wanted him to stay here.'

'What's this Juganet thing then?' said Jane.

'I dunno… sounds daft.'

'Then there's this force he keeps on about. Is it human or somethin'?'

'He said it'd been made manifest, whatever that means,' he shrugged.

When Roy left his father with Goodchild, he didn't go to his room. He'd decided to go out of the house to meet up with Arby and Jane, but without alarming his father, so he left by the conservatory door and then made his way around to the front of the house, towards the Vennor's cottage.

Goodchild was prowling around upstairs in the Briggs's house. He tried several doors before settling on one… He went in to the room and stared hard at the wall… which suddenly became transparent, like a window into the house next door. Goodchild could now see the weakened Sky, lying on the bed in the Vennor's house. Goodchild was pleased with the result and allowed himself the thinnest of smiles at his achievement.

In the spare room next door, Sky became restless, as if he could feel the presence of Goodchild.

Jane and Arby were still sitting on the stairs outside the

boxroom, where they'd put Sky, when there was a knock at the door. Jane and Arby exchanged worried looks, not knowing what to expect after all the strange events they'd experienced in the past hours.

'Don't answer it,' warned Jane.

'I got to.'

'Find out who it is first.'

Arby got up and went down to answer the door.

Jane followed him.

Arby put his ear to the door and called, 'Who is it?'

'It's me!' replied Roy from outside the door.

They let him in. They were both relieved to hear a voice they recognised.

'Thanks,' said Roy. 'How's your mother?'

'Taken her to hospital for X-rays,' said Jane.

'What d'you want then?' Arby asked irritably.

Roy shifted uneasily. 'Nothing.' He waited a second or two before telling them about what happened. 'Only... I went back to the school.'

'So?' snorted Arby.

'There was this strange bloke down there, in the library.'

'Who? What was he doing?' asked Jane.

Arby supplied the answer. 'Nosing I expect.' Then to Roy. 'Just like you.'

'Anyway, the thing is, he's turned up at our place, and Dad seems to know him.'

'So?'

'Well, he's a weird sort of bloke. Ambrose Goodchild.'

The odd, uncommon name caused Jane to give a burst of laughter. 'Ambrose?'

'You wouldn't laugh if you saw him,' cautioned Roy.

'Why? What does he look like?

Goodchild, his face screwed up with rage, began an attack on the comatose Sky through the wall.

He swirled his cloak like a madman and summoned up the wind…

The window slammed open under his power, then leaves and twigs appeared from nowhere and began to swirl in through the window and settle around Sky. A sort of green lichen appeared on his cheek… then it started to spread over his face…

Goodchild continued his attack until Sky became literally covered in organic matter, the leafy detritus of Autumn and the spreading silver-green lichen.

Sky was aware of the attack, but he was still very weak. Then from somewhere, deep in his psyche, he managed to find the willpower to resist. He slowly raised his hands so that they protruded from his leafy tomb. It looked as if Sky might be ready to defend himself…

Goodchild reacted and built up his frantic attack. The gale began to get stronger and the wild swirling wind became so strong that it caused the bedside lamp to crash down and a metal fan heater topple over on to the floor with a bang!

The noise attracted the kids. They rushed upstairs to Sky's bedroom. Arby hammered on the spare room door then tried the handle. The door appeared to be stuck.

'Give us a hand here, Roy.'

He and Roy pushed hard against it with their shoulders and finally burst through, where they saw Sky, yet again covered in a mound of leaves and twigs.

'Sky!' shouted Arby.

The children gathered around him.

He spoke falteringly. 'I… am… sorry…'

Jane and Arby started to clear the heaps of leaves from him and straightened the bed.

Roy was watching, confused and afraid. 'What was it?' Where did all this stuff come from?'

'I dunno,' said Arby.

'Some sort of force,' interjected Jane, guessing, but her look showed she wasn't at all sure she was right.

'Force?' said Roy.

'Yeah, things try to smother him… devour him… living things. This Goodchild is part of it,' said Arby with some conviction.

Roy is incredulous 'Eh? You're joking?'

'Never mind,' grunted Arby.

Jane appealed to Roy. 'Can you get your father's car?'

Roy frowned, as he wondered what for.

'To get him to a hospital. Arby can drive it.'

'Better hurry up,' urged Arby. 'He could die!'

Roy nodded and went out.

Chapter Six
'What Dread Hand'

MAJOR BRIGGS WAS SITTING in the lounge staring into space. His drink, untouched, was still in his hand. He was in some kind of a kind of trance.

Roy came in, looked at him and shouted, 'Dad?'

The Major registered the voice and blinked, then began to come round. His eyes gradually focused on Roy, who was standing in front of him.

'I'm borrowing the car, Dad.' It was a simple statement of fact rather than a request.

The Major, still mystified by events, looked around the room for Goodchild. 'Where – where's Ambrose?'

Roy, seeing his father was in a kind of stupor, decided to take his chance and swooped on his father's car keys lying on the table. 'It's alright, Dad. Why not have a nap? It'd do you good.'

The Major was now beginning to realise what was happening. 'What're you doing? Where are you going with my keys?'

Roy thought quickly. 'It's Mrs Vennor. Look, I'm going to the hospital.'

'What? The hospital?'

'Yes, It's Mrs Vennor. She's had an accident. Jane and Arby have got to be there. Ok?'

The Major tried to get up out of his chair, but fell back as if utterly exhausted. 'Look… son… I don't know if…' he uttered feebly.

Roy decided to make a swift exit before his father could object. 'It's an emergency, Dad. I'll drop them off and I'll be back soon,' he called from downstairs, just before slamming the front door.

The Major seemed satisfied by the explanation and slumped back into his chair again. The faraway look returned to his eyes.

Sky was being whisked through the hospital corridor on a trolley. Arby, Jane and Roy followed, trying to keep up. A nurse kept an oxygen mask pressed to Sky's face as they approached a door with the sign 'Intensive Care Unit' above it. The doors swung open and Sky was taken in.

The nurse turned and raised her hand to stop the three kids. 'Sorry, you can't come in,' she said. 'We'll keep you informed.'

The doors closed on them.

*

Doctor Saul, an eager-looking man in his forties, and three nurses, hovered busily around Sky, putting an adrenalin drip into him.

One nurse adjusted the oxygen levels and tried to take his pulse. She had a worried look, which the doctor picked up on. He looked anxiously over at the TV monitor for a reading. A flat line…

Sky appeared to have no pulse.

The doctor stopped in his tracks, lowered his mask, and looked as if he was about to make a sad pronouncement when a beep was heard from the monitor. It was followed by a series of beeps, and peaks began to show up on the screen.

Doctor Saul looked down at his patient amazed, as Sky removed his oxygen mask and whispered to him. 'Juganet… is this… Juganet?'

Doctor Saul bent over him and strained to hear what he was saying. He turned to one of the nurses. 'Did you get that, Staff Nurse?'

She shook her head.

Roy returned home to find that his father was quiet, completely absorbed in his own thoughts. In fact, the Major was feeling somewhat embarrassed by previous events, and avoided eye contact with Roy. He was still sitting in the chair, as he had when he faced Goodchild.

He decided to take on a friendly, more inclusive, approach towards Roy. 'Well, Roy. What d'you think, eh? I must be going round the twist… or something?' He shook his head.

Roy appreciated the tone, and he too was friendlier

towards his dad, and said, without a hint of sarcasm, 'Would you like another drink, Dad?'

The Major considered this for a moment. 'Yes... yes. Good, thanks.' As Roy poured him a gin and tonic, the Major rose, moved toward Roy and began to think out loud. 'Far as I remember, Ambrose was a thick set little man. Ruddy complexion, yes. REME if I remember correctly, met him down in Devizes... Yes, that's the feller.'

Roy cut a slice of lemon and popped it in the drink. 'Who?'

'Goodchild. Wasn't a tall thin... I wonder how I ever came to think it was him? Anyway he's dead and buried. I should know, I went to his bally funeral.' He accepted the drink from Roy with a nod and went on. 'He's been dead for years.' He found it difficult to get his head round the idea. But went on trying. 'Goodchild. Goodchild...'

Roy too, was concerned about Goodchild's strange visitation and the whole evening's events. He decided not to press his father for more details.

Jane and Arby were waiting anxiously in the hospital reception area for any news of Sky. Jane nervously dug her thumbnails into her empty styrene cup.

The door from the wards opened, and a bright and breezy Doctor Saul came in. He was holding a clipboard.

'Hello!' he said with a sideways smile. He took a seat in front of them. 'Now, I want you two to tell me everything you can remember about your friend and this fall of his. Right?'

Arby and Jane nodded but remained silent.

The doctor held his pen above a report sheet, ready to

write. He couldn't quite understand why they were being so reticent. Pretty straightforward surely, he thought.

'Well, come along.'

Still nothing from them, they were both tight lipped.

He began to wonder if they were perhaps handicapped in some way, but immediately put that thought aside. They were obviously just being awkward – or there was something of a criminal nature involved?

'Come on. Anything,' he said. Then he became even more suspicious. 'You were actually *there*? Weren't you?'

Arby nodded and then Jane spluttered. 'He...'

Having ventured an answer, Arby relied on her to carry on. He signalled with his eyes that the ball was in her court.

'He... went up to bed, like... and uh... when we went up, he was lying on the bed... sort of.'

'No blow, then? Didn't fall out of bed or anything? Was he unconscious?' enquired the doctor.

'No,' said Jane emphatically.

Arby spoke up to help her out, and made up something that might sound plausible. 'He said he had a nightmare.'

Doctor Saul smiled encouragingly.

Arby's story trailed off lamely. 'Then he just passed out...'

The doctor sighed heavily. Then tried a different tack. 'Has he had any previous history? I mean, has he ever done anything like this before?'

Arby almost put his foot in it. 'Well only when that... No.' He shut himself up.

The doctor pursued him for answers. 'Come on, you've got to help me here. He was saying something... Juganet?'

Arby and Jane exchanged glances under the doctor's watchful eyes.

'Mean anything to you? He ever say anything like that to you?'

Arby and Jane answer together, emphatically, 'No.'

The doctor decided to appear to take them into his confidence. He lowered his voice. 'Now listen, if you want me to help him – and he is seriously ill, very seriously ill – I must know the truth. Is that clear?'

Arby and Jane nodded.

'Right. What is it? This Juganet?'

Arby and Jane were under intense pressure but remained silent.

Doctor Saul nodded. 'Thank you,' he snapped. He was completely amazed by their attitude and it struck him again that there might be something more sinister than a nightmare… But, although he found their evasion rather strange, he decided he should put it down to sullen teenage angst.

He moved to the door. As it opened, he allowed some people coming through the other way to pass him. It was Mr and Mrs Vennor.

Jim Vennor had a broad smile on his face. 'How d'you get here?' he said.

Jane crossed him. 'You alright, mum?'

'Perfectly. You didn't need to come love. Don't know what all the fuss was about.'

'Best to be sure though, Joyce, eh?' said Vennor.

'Doc Marshall's giving us a lift. I expect he can find some room for you. You comin' back with us?'

Arby and Jane looked at each other. They shrugged.

'No, it's alright. We'll come back later,' said Arby.

'As you wish,' said Vennor.

'We'll get the bus,' said Jane.

Joyce turned back to Arby. 'What about your friend? He still at home is he?'

Arby had to think quickly and came up with. 'Oh… no mum, he had to get a move on… didn't want to put you out or anythin', so he got the Bristol bus.'

Joyce frowned. 'Oh, well he'd have been welcome, you know that.'

John took her by the arm and guided her away.

'Glad to hear you're OK, Mum,' said Arby as they went though the exit door.

Jane and Arby sighed with relief, they'd managed to get around some awkward questioning. Then John came back in and faced them and they got worried again.

He put his hand into his trouser pocket and pulled out some change. 'Got enough for the bus fare have you?'

'Yes, Dad. Don't worry now. You get home with Mum,' said a relieved Arby.

In Intensive Care, Sky appeared to be asleep, but the pinging of the heart monitor got his attention. He turned his head to watch it.

The normal slow moving line, with a peak on each heartbeat, had somehow made itself into a jumbled pattern of lines – a bit like spaghetti, but moving like a tangle of elvers or worms.

Sky stared at it.

'Who's there? Who can hear me?' he said softly.

There was an answer from the monitor, a voice with

a strong South Wales accent. 'Hello… Hello.' This was followed by a warm chuckle.

In the corridor outside, a man in his sixties was wheeling a tea trolley. He was balding and wore a greying beard. He was dressed in pyjamas and an oversize plaid dressing gown, denoting that he was a patient in the hospital.

He looked up at the ceiling as he spoke, ecstatic that he was able to hear a voice. I knew it, he thought. Now they gotta believe me. Here, clear as day in the damn 'ospital!

'Hello… Hello, I can hear you mun. I can hear you.' He chuckled to himself again. 'That was clever… Call me Tom, but I cannot bear being called Tommy, OK?'

The 'Tommy' thing had caused him some bother in the past, as certain kinds of people would use it to tease him. Then he'd get mad and start yelling. That's when they'd give him pills that made him sad…

Tom had what's called special needs. He'd been unable to make any headway at school, and no one had been able to find out what was wrong. Whatever it was that ailed him, Tom heard voices – and had done since he was a child. He was presently undergoing a long series of psychological tests by neurology specialists, which included regular brain scans to try and find out more about his condition.

He was supposed to stay in his ward, in bed, but he was easily bored. Since Tom was an amiable soul, he was allowed to move around the wards in the hospital and very soon became everybody's pal. The nurses all put up with him and his strange ways, and the administrator had given him permission to take the tea trolley around the wards twice a day.

Tom wheeled the trolley on down the corridor. He was very pleased with himself at hearing the voices. 'Go on… Go on. Do it again,' he said.

A nursing sister came towards him and saw him talking to the ceiling. 'You alright, Tom?' she said with a smile. 'Made contact again have you? Who is it this time?'

'Shhh! Shhush a minute. You'll be able to hear 'em for yourself.' He scanned the ceiling again for the voices.

The nurse smiled and went on her way.

When she'd gone, he looked up at the ceiling again. 'Are you still there? Ohh. T'was Sister, t'was Sister.' He stroked his beard in contemplation, then looked up again enthusiastically. 'It's getting clearer, it's getting louder.' He scanned the doors in the corridor, then made off towards the door to Intensive Care, still in conversation with the disembodied voice he was hearing. 'Yes, of course… what d'you want? Juganet? No, never heard of it… Wait. I tell you what, do me a picture of it.' He pointed at the blank wall of the hospital corridor.

He looked at the blank wall and obviously saw an image on it. He laughed with real pleasure.

'Hey, that's good, that's clever… goin' round isn't it.' He made a circular movement with his hand. 'Like a circus.' He was then attracted to the wall again. 'Oh, look at them colours… Oh, it's lovely they are… It's fire is it?'

Then, with a self-satisfied chuckle, Tom hinted at, perhaps, something secret in his past… He remembered a time when he was in a barn full of hay and he was holding a box of matches… He struck a match…

'I do like fires.'

A door opened and Doctor Saul came out.

Tom drew Doctor Saul's attention to the apparition he could see on the wall.

'Doctor Saul, look at these flames.'

Saul briefly tried to seem interested, then looked at his watch. 'Yes, but I'm busy, Tom. I'll talk to you later in one our sessions alright?'

In his room, Sky could hear Tom's voice on the monitor. 'Look, Doctor! Look! Can't you see it?'

Out in the corridor, Tom was somewhat deflated by Doctor Saul's lack of interest and blamed him for making the vision disappear.

'You made it go, didn't you! It was all goin' round and you made it go. Say you're sorry now.'

'I'm sorry, Tom,' said Saul.

'I should think so indeed.' Tom wheeled his trolley away, still looking up at the ceiling. 'Go on, do it again. Do those circles again…'

Both Jane and Arby had noted Tom's childlike behaviour, and they somehow had the feeling that it might be connected to Sky.

They were keen to talk to him, but Sky came first.

'Can we see our friend now?' Jane asked Doctor Saul.

'In the morning… tomorrow.' His emergency bleeper went off. 'Excuse me, please.' The doctor rushed off, leaving Arby and Jane frustrated.

Doctor Saul went into Intensive Care, where a nurse was attending Sky. She had a puzzled look on her face.

Saul noticed. 'What is it? What's the matter?'

'It's gone now.'

'What?'

'The EEG.' She turned to the screen, which was functioning normally. She felt a bit stupid – like crying wolf. 'It's gone now. I called in to see the patient, everything was normal, but when I looked at the screen... I've never seen anything like it.'

'Like what?'

'A pattern I suppose, a moving circular sort of pattern, glowing and pulsing and changing all the time. Then it stopped. Suddenly.'

Saul was studying the EEG paper printout intently.

There were some very high peaks on it.

The nurse pointed out where the activity ended. 'There you see.'

'Get me the other notes please, Nurse.'

She nodded and left. Saul became thoughtful. This was most interesting, something quite unique... and stimulated by the patient himself by the look of things. Wow! I've got to tell Brandt about this, he thought.

He dug deep into his top pocket and produced a card with a number on it. He moved to the wall telephone, dialled the number and studied the printout as he waited for an answer.

'Hello, Professor Brandt? Hope I'm not disturbing you. It's, ah... Doctor Saul, Denton Saul here. Avoncrest Hospital. We met at the University last month. I did a lecture on psychosurgery, yes?'

Professor Brandt, in his fifties, with short grey hair and a goatee beard, was speaking to Saul from behind his elaborate oak desk in the university campus. His window looked out over the red-brick walls of other departments in the university.

'Psychosurgery? Ah, yes, of course I remember. You were doing a paper on it, weren't you? That's right. I found it most intriguing, Doctor. So what can I do for you?'

'Oh… Well it's something I've come across here at the hospital that I thought might be of special interest…'

'Mmm. Tell me more.'

'Well, it's case of mine.'

'So, how is it special?'

Doctor Saul had to look at his notes to quote them. 'Oh, yes… Well, Professor, we've got unconsciousness, rigidity of the body and possible seizure.'

'Mmmmm. Strikes me it could be like catalepsy?'

'Yes, it looks very much like catalepsy…' replied Saul.

Sky was fully awake now. He sat up on the bed and looked over at Doctor Saul, listening to what he was saying on the telephone.

'… but with the possibility that trance has been self-induced.'

The professor now showed a real interest. 'What? Really? You mean? Tell me more young man.'

Saul now began to grin, highly delighted to get the professor interested in his work. 'Yes, well, the other feature that might be of particular interest you, Professor, is the amount of transmission taking place… Aha… Well, the instruments are registering a whole series of definite signals from the patient himself.'

Saul looked round at Sky and saw the monitor screen showing the circling shapes.

'Excuse me Professor, but it's happening now. You really should see this.'

'Yes, of course. When shall I come?'

'Could you come over right away?'

'Sadly no, I've got a few bits and bobs to do here. Reports to go through. But I'll be there as soon as I finish them. Shouldn't be too long, an hour or so –'

'That's great. Soon as you finish then, that's really super and I assure you it'll be very much worth your while. Right up your neurological street as it were.'

The professer had a smile as he signed off. 'I'll be as quick as I can. And thank you, Doctor Saul, for thinking of me. It sounds really interesting. I can't wait.'

'See you later then. Cheers.' Doctor Saul replaced the receiver, wearing a satisfied grin – perhaps rather pleased he would be able to get out of the office for an hour or two. He moved over to Sky and looked at the patterns on the screen, then checked the printout again.

Sky, meanwhile, had his palms facing his eyes. He called out telepathically. 'Tom! Help me! I am in danger!'

Tom's answer came back the in same way. 'What? You want a biscuit?'

When he heard Sky's voice, Tom was on a ward, pouring a cup of tea for a patient. He handed the tea over speedily, then reversed his trolley and went out to the corridor. He wheeled it down toward Sky's room.

'Tell you what… I'm doin' my tea round at the minute, won't be long. Then I'll come back and help you… Alright?' He stopped and faced the wall, full of anticipation. 'Hey, show us the pictures.'

Sky obliged Tom, who was delighted by the show on the wall in front of him.

'Oh… fantastic…' Then Tom looked up towards the ceiling and saw another image. 'Hey, why are those stones on fire? I seen some stones on fire once. We had an outin' once, when I was a boy. They all thought I was mad, 'cause I was the only one that seen 'em burnin', see?' He described a circle with his hand. 'In a big circle… like wagons.'

'Where?' demanded Sky. 'Where did you see them?'

Tom cringed from Sky's sharp, tone. 'No, no! I can't remember,' he cringed as he pushed his trolley off down to another ward with a sudden change of mood, a sort of servile acceptance of his lowly post. 'After all,' thought Tom. 'I'm doing my best. I got to do me round.'

He moved further down the corridor and into the reception area. It was there that he ran his trolley over the toes of a tall, imposing figure in a pinstriped suit.

Tom looked up at him. 'Want a cuppa tea, mister?' he asked innocently.

The man ignored Tom and went up to the receptionist.

Tom called after him, incensed by the man's surly attitude. 'Hey, say you're sorry, you!'

The receptionist butted in. 'Come on Tommy, back up the wards.'

'Don't you call me *Tommy*!' Tom said pointing his finger at her angrily.

'Get on then – Tom – scoot.' She turned back to the tall man. 'I'm sorry. Yes, Sir. Can I help you?'

'Doctor Saul please. Professor Brandt sent me.' He gave her a thin sinister smile.

She lifted the phone, pressed in a number and asked, 'What name shall I say sir?

'Goodchild.'

In the Intensive Care ward, Sky was fully aware of Goodchild's presence, but he was unable to move. He couldn't get away from his mortal enemy...

Roy was cleaning a cylinder head with a wire brush, talking to Arby and Jane in their garage–cum-workshop. Having been told they definitely couldn't see Sky until the morning, Arby and Jane had got the bus home. They were now listening intently to Roy.

'Then Dad said this bloke Ambrose had been dead for years... So who is he, if he's not Ambrose Goodchild? And why is he after Sky?'

During the ensuing silence, as they mulled this over, Roy continued to clean rust from the cylinder head.

Jane, who was sitting on an old car seat next to Roy, piped up, sounding all knowledgeable. 'Look, Sky's from another time. Right?'

'Oh, come on. Another *time*? He's really pulled the wool over your eyes,' said Roy dismissively, taking the wind out of her sails.

'It's one force against another force,' said Arby. 'It's like the body. It's like nature – resisting disease.'

Roy thought this over, then made a face. 'Antibodies you mean?'

Arby looked blank. 'Somethin' like that, yeah.'

'OK. So, Sky's the disease?' said Roy.

Arby considered Roy's comment.

'Well, Sky's the intruder… yes.'

'So why help him? Why not this Goodchild?'

Arby shrugged. 'Didn't know about him, did I?'

Roy started to check the spark plugs from his bike, then looked up at them again. Still intent on playing Devil's Advocate. 'Anyway how d'you know Sky's not doing the same thing to you that Goodchild did to my dad?'

Again Arby considered his answer before speaking. 'Look. All Sky wants… All Sky wants is to get away. To find this Juganet and get away.'

Jane chipped in. 'Sky's needed.'

Roy wasn't so sure. 'So he says.' He carried on with his work then asked, 'Alright then, suppose there is such a thing as a Juganet. Suppose he can move through time, suppose he is needed… What I'm asking is, what for?'

Jane strained to recall the words Sky had said to her in the tunnel. '"I suppose, in your terms, I am to be a god." That's what he told me.'

Sky now had sensors attached to his forehead. He was totally alone and looked terribly vulnerable.

The door opened slowly… It was Tom. He slinked in, very nervous, knowing himself to be out of bounds.

'Not supposed to be in here. What d'you bring me in here for?' He approached Sky's bed. Then his mood changed again. A broad grin appeared on his face. 'Hey, show me them burnin' stones again.'

There was no response from Sky.

'Here, I'll give you as bit of chocolate. Here you are.' Tom dug into his dressing-gown pocket and brought out a bar of chocolate.

Sky pushed himself up slowly from the bed and then tore away the little round plasters holding the sensors to his forehead.

Tom was distraught. 'Hey! You're not supposed to do that. They'll blame me for that, man!'

Sky finally got himself upright in the bed. He confided in Tom, 'There is someone in this building who means to harm me.'

Tom began to grin and nod sagely. Paranoia was something he definitely understood. 'Oh they're always at it. That's what they do in here, man.'

'I… I can't focus Tom. Switch off the machine.'

'No, no, not allowed.'

Sky got face-to-face with Tom and willed him to help.

'Will you show me the pictures if I do?'

'Very well.'

Tom went over to unplug the monitor, then went back to Sky. 'Not fire, is it? More like rays, like, innit?' He screwed his eyes shut, waiting for the images to appear in his mind.

'First you must show me a picture.'

'No, I can't.'

'Yes, you can, Tom… Concentrate. I cannot see clearly.' Sky placed his hands above the man's eyes. 'Concentrate Tom. Who did you see? The man at the door. What did he look like? Concentrate!'

Tom was in turmoil as he tried to project the image to Sky. He squeezed the sides of his head with effort.

'Concentrate!' begged Sky.

Tom was exhausted.

Then suddenly Sky picked up the image of Goodchild. He immediately started to move out of his bed.

'What's the matter?' asked Tom.

'I must… get away… I…'

'Hey, hey, you're not supposed to do that, man. You'll get germs!'

Sky put his arms out for Tom to assist him.

Tom was too scared and confused to do anything. 'No, no. I gotta go! Shouldn't be in 'ere by rights, anyhow.' The thought of retribution, in the form of denying him to do the tea round, was massive in his eyes. Tom began to jibber. Then he turned and rushed out of the room.

Sky collapsed, half in and half out of his bed.

Doctor Saul and Goodchild were walking down the hospital corridor on their way to see Sky.

'Pity Brandt couldn't make it,' said Saul.

'Yes, isn't it?' Goodchild smiled effusively.

'Have you been with the research team long, Doctor… er, um?' Saul had forgotten his name.

'Goodchild. I was with the Professor in Stockholm.'

'And do you share his views?'

'We must all do what we can to ease the burden of pain, Doctor Saul. Mental pain and anguish can be among the worst of agonies to the sufferers.'

Doctor Saul was a little narked that Brandt had sent someone else and furthermore he wasn't sure he was too fond of this gentleman. Saul had been angling to get a research post with Brandt, but obviously the Professor wasn't that keen.

Saul opened the door into his office, ushered Goodchild in, then went to find his notes.

Goodchild was a little annoyed to find himself in Saul's

office. He began to speak with apparent authority. 'I must see the patient. In a case such as this, immediate surgery is often the only solution.'

Doctor Saul challenged him. 'Oh? You think so? What about other forms of therapy?'

Goodchild almost snatched the notes from Saul. 'Are these the notes?' He scanned them too quickly to have read them.

'Oh, yes. Ah… feelings of persecution… a sense of being special, it's a typical case of messianic fantasy compensating for social rejection, the old god-from-outer-space thing.'

Goodchild gave him a knowing look, then returned to the notes.

Saul continued to fill him in. 'The only other interesting thing is this paranormal anxiety during self-induced trance, as if he were trying to… contact someone.'

In his room, Sky, helpless on the hospital bed, called urgently in his mind, 'Arby! Arby! Help me! Help me! Arby! Jane! Help me!'

Another person, who received Sky's urgent telepathic pleas for help was Tom. He was in the corridor, scared and crumpled up in a corner, trying to shield himself from Sky's plaintive calls.

He shouted to the ceiling, 'Oh, stop it! Leave me alone! Stop it! I tried, but I can't do nothin', I can't, I can't, I can't.' He plugged his ears with his fingers in the hope that he could defy Sky's voice.

A passing nurse stopped and wondered what was causing Tom's agony. 'Tom? What is it? What's happened?'

'It's him. He keeps on shoutin' at me, he won't stop.'

The nurse looked around and saw nothing. 'Now Tom, there's no-one here.' She held his shoulders gently. 'No-one can harm you.'

Tom calmed down a bit.

She remembered Tom's symptoms, and adopted a caring tone. 'Hearing voices again, is it Tom? Now why don't you go back to bed, you'll be better get off there… I'll bring you some medicine, something to calm you down, shall I?'

Tom looked around warily. 'Will it stop him?'

'Come on Tom. Let's get you back to your ward.'

Tom allowed the nurse to guide him back towards his ward.

In the garage, Arby was still with Roy, helping him with his engine. Roy held the cylinder head in place while Arby tightened the bolts up with a spanner.

Suddenly Arby and Jane heard a wild jangling noise in their head. It was so powerful that they had to hold their heads in their hands. They could hardly bear it.

Roy was completely flummoxed. 'What's the matter?' he said.

'Can't you hear it?' shouted Arby.

'Hear what?'

'It's Sky!' screamed Jane.

'Sky?' asked Roy.

Arby made for the Land Rover, followed by Jane who, in her frantic rush, scrabbled in through the back door, it being the nearest.

Roy stared at them in utter amazement. 'Hey, where you going?'

Arby started the Land Rover and they roared off in a cloud of diesel exhaust.

Roy was left standing there watching them go.

In the office, Goodchild glared down at Doctor Saul, who was sitting at the desk and said forcefully, 'Operate.'

'But you don't seem to realise –'

'Operate… Now!'

Saul began to wonder how Brandt had any time for this guy. He was so old fashioned! We don't do trepanning any more, he thought, as he counted off the objections on his fingers. 'A: no permission, and B: no need. And if we do what you suggest, he'll likely end up as a cabbage.'

'You agreed the condition is critical.'

'Not necessarily no…'

'Doctor Saul.' Goodchild stared directly into Saul's face.

Saul stared back with unblinking eyes, transfixed.

Goodchild then spoke to him slowly and calmly. 'Doctor Saul… you agreed the condition was critical…'

Saul was still looking at him, eyes fixed on Goodchild's. 'I… I agree…'

Goodchild moved forward and stood over him willing him to obey. 'Without emergency measures…'

Saul repeated the words. 'Without… emergency… measures…'

'There is no hope.'

'There is… no hope…'

'Of saving the patient.'

'Of saving… the patient.'

There was a knock on the door, and the sister popped her head around the door. 'Doctor Saul?'

Before she could say any more, Goodchild informed her with quiet emphasis what she should do. 'Sister… Sister… Doctor Saul will be assisting me in an operation… Please have the theatre made ready as soon as possible.'

The sister too was quickly under Goodchild's powerful telepathic influence. 'Yes, of course. As soon as possible, yes.'

As she left, the strange unearthly breeze that usually accompanied Goodchild began to whip up in Saul's office. It blew papers all over the office, but Doctor Saul was quite oblivious to it. He was still rooted to his chair in a trance…

Sky had revived a little and saw Tom standing at his bedside, attempting to pull out the adrenalin drip lead.

Sky became aware of him and warned him, 'Tom, hide!'

'What?'

'They'll see you, Tom. Hide!'

'You, makin' me do things,' whined Tom.

He ran and hid in the toilet, just as the sister and a nurse entered with a hospital surgery trolley bed.

The sister was amazed to see the state of Sky, across the bed and uncovered. 'What on Earth are you doing?'

'You must not help them,' Sky whispered telepathically to Tom.

The sister lifted Sky back on to the operating bed. 'Let's get you back into bed, shall we?'

Tom, in hiding, continued to hear Sky's voice sound in his brain. 'You must not help them… You must understand… Tom, you know what you must do.'

'Oh damn,' said Tom in his agony.

*

Meanwhile, Goodchild had got dressed in cap, mask and gown. He was putting rubber gloves on, prior to the operation on Sky.

He turned to one of the nurses and said, 'Is everything prepared?'

'Yes Doctor.'

'Then you may bring the patient.'

In the busy reception area, a tannoy voice boomed out, 'Doctor Voisey to Casualty, please. Doctor Voisey to Casualty.'

gerly awaiting his patient. The trolley carrying Sky was wheeled in to him… and the doors closed behind them. The lighted sign 'Operating' was on…

Arby and Jane searched the corridors, looking for Sky. They stopped when the reached the operating theatre.

'He's got 'im. Nothing we can do,' said Arby grimly.

In the theatre, Goodchild moved to the operating table. Sky's head was now covered in a blue plastic cap and the sheet covered him up to the eyes.

As the anaesthetist put the mask on the patient's face, Goodchild took it from her roughly and pressed it down hard over the patient's mouth. He glared down at his victim, then grinned with anticipation… Goodchild began forcing the mask harder on to the patient's mouth, then he suddenly stopped. He angrily pulled the sheet away from the face to reveal… a petrified Tom.

'He told me to! He made me!' yelped Tom.

Goodchild, irate, bundled the mask and tubes on the sister and raged out. 'Fools!'

Tom looked around balefully at the operating team, fearful of some kind of punishment. 'Not goin' to hurt me are you?' mumbled Tom. 'Was 'im… No blame attaches… eh?'

The operating team were as amazed as anyone to see Tom.

The anaesthatist looked at him angrily. 'What d'you think you're up to, Tom?'

'It was 'im I tell you. Made me he did.'

Goodchild stormed into the Intensive Care unit, where Sky had been. He went up to the bed, which appeared to have someone lying in it, and swept the bedclothes back to reveal pillows placed to look like a body.

Goodchild slowly rose, glaring up at the ceiling, then disappeared into thin air…

Chapter Seven
'And Did Those Feet?'

ARBY AND JANE WERE WAITING in the corridor when they heard Tom, still talking to a disembodied Sky as he left the operating theatre.

'No, no, I can't... I'm not s'posed to go outside the 'ospital grounds! S'posed to go back to bed now!'

Arby approached Tom, who was still wearing the operation gown and plastic cap. Arby touched his arm then spoke to him softly. 'Tom, alright, don't worry Tom. Where is he?'

'Who? Tom was suspicious of these strangers.

'You were talking to him,' said Jane. She calmed Tom down by taking his hands in hers. 'Please, where is he? He's our friend.'

Tom whispered into her ear conspiratorially. 'He wants me to go with him see, an' I don't want to go.' He suddenly clapped his hands over his ears. Sky was invading his brain, putting pressure on him. 'No, no, don't make me please.'

The Vennor's Land Rover, headlights glaring, was speeding through the night. It went from tree-lined back roads to a main road, the A38, heading towards Bridgwater.

Inside, Arby and Jane were in the front with Tom and Sky was in the back…

Sky was looking at the distraught Tom who, though swathed in a blanket, was shivering with fear. He knew he would be in for it when he got back.

Sky addressed him with due respect for what he'd done. 'Thank you Tom… I'm sorry… I had to…'

'But they'll attach blame…'

'No, they will not harm you. I promise.'

But Tom was consumed with worry that the hospital authorities would extract some kind of retribution. In fact he feared the worst. 'They won't let me take the tea round… if I don't go back. Let me go back, eh?'

'I need you,' said Sky, then added quite sharply. 'Now be quiet.'

Overhearing this, Jane turned to Sky. 'Why did you bring him?' she said.

'Tom is one of the few… His mind is not cluttered and patterned like yours. Its doors are open. He can see what I see. He will interpret that to you.'

Jane frowned and proceeded carefully, not wishing to offend Tom. 'But, he's supposed to be… simple isn't he?'

'No. It is you who are complicated.'

*

Major Briggs was talking on the telephone to the police.

'Yes… ahum… hm… hm… They've done what?'

Simmonds was on the other end of the line at his desk, sounding very serious. 'Well, they've only snatched the young blond boy practically from the operatin' table, oh, and it seems they've taken an old gentleman… He's sort of… of a, well, you know… simple fellow. I've had to get Avon and Somerset Constabulary in. Out of my hands now. What about your lad? He throw any light on where they might have gone?'

Roy came in and sat on the arm of an easy chair. The Major registered him and covered the mouthpiece of the phone. 'D'you know anything about this?'

'About what?'

'They've done a bunk, they've taken your friend from the hospital – and another nutter. They say anything to you?'

Roy opened a magazine as usual, and made it look as if he was reading.

'It's the po-lice again.' The Major put a heavy emphasis on the word.

'They just split, Dad.'

'What?'

Roy answered as if to a child. 'Rushed off. It was Arby's idea, nothing to do with me.'

The Major returned to his phone conversation. 'Hello? Just checking. No, he's been here with me all evening. Knows nothing about it. Nothing at all…' Then he remarked wearily. 'Yes Sergeant, don't worry, I'll pass it on to the Vennors. Goodbye.' He replaced the receiver and gave vent to his feelings about the local constabulary. 'Damn peasant, that man, Sergeant Whatsisname.' The Major moved to pour himself another drink.

Arby drove the Land Rover off the main road into a narrow country road. They passed a sign for Charterhouse. It was a walled road and well off the beaten track.

In the Land Rover, Sky scanned the area with his eyes, and appeared to pick something up.

He called to Arby, 'Arby... slow now... There is safety somewhere here.... .Tom, what is this?'

Tom concentrated and then started to see a vision.

'It's... it's a children's place. Happy they are. Singin' too.'

Arby stopped the Land Rover and they looked out at a small, Victorian village school, with simple arched windows and a miniscule bell tower. They got out and approached the heavy wooden front door.

Sky held out his hand and directed his energy on the door lock. In a few seconds it clicked open...

Arby opened the door and entered, followed by Jane. He found the light switches and turned them on. It was a small Junior school with tiny children's desks and mini chairs in groups. Pinned on the walls were children's paintings and some alphabet boards and some pictures taken from magazines of animals, mostly. The most striking thing about the place was that all around the walls like a frieze above the picture rail, writ large, were the words of a hymn done in Gothic script style. It read:

'All things bright and beautiful, all creatures great and small, all things wise and wonderful, the Lord God made them all.'

Tom was being very cautious, and waited in the hall until

he got the feel of the place. Then a beaming smile came to his face and he entered. 'Caaw, that's good.'

He stood with Jane and Arby as they looked around at the whole four walls of lettering. They were sure they could hear faraway children's ghostly voices singing the hymn.

Sky was suddenly in the room. There appeared to be a kind of aura around him as he listened to the echoing 'voices' singing.

'All things bright and beautiful,
 All creatures great and small,
 All things wild and wonderful,
 The Lord God made them all…'

Sky looked around at the paintings and the pictures. One of them took his interest, and he stood looking at it with a quizzical look on his face. It was a print of a pre-raphaelite painting by Holman Hunt. The picture's title was in the margin of the frame. It read: 'Jesus, Light Of The World'. It depicted Christ, in a dark wood, holding a lantern and lighting the way.

'Is this the Lord God?' mused Sky.

'Well, sort of,' ventured Jane.

'That's Jesus, Son of God,' confirmed Arby.

'Which God?' asked Sky.

At which Tom began to sing softly. 'Immortal, Invisible, God only wise….' He continued humming the verse.

'Then this is one of your religions,' said Sky. 'I am safe then? When did he arrive?'

'Jesus? Well. He was born two thousand years ago.'

'Born?' Sky seemed utterly amazed.

Tom shuffled forward. He seemed to be in deep thought and said, 'Like one of them burnin' circles, innit?'

'Tell them,' said Sky. 'Describe it to them, make them understand.'

Tom fixed his jaw, full of determination. Trying to find the words.

Sky turned to Arby and Jane and said, 'I am safe now. Speak to Tom.'

Arby and Jane tried to fit on the tiny chairs.

Tom drew up a chair. 'Ask me questions. Go on…'

There was a long pause as they tried to think of what to say. Jane finally broke the silence. 'How d'you know what's goin' on? How do you see what Sky sees?'

'Oh, s'easy innit? I do know. I do see pictures, see.'

'What d'you mean?' said Jane.

'These circles,' said Arby. 'You talk about circles, don't you? When you talk to Sky?'

'The burnin' ones?' Tom's eyes look beyond them and he pointed to the wall. 'There's one over there, see.'

They swing around to see a mural depicting an angel with a fiery halo.

Tom started to laugh. 'But they're not on fire, are they really?'

Arby leaned forward to Tom and said, 'Could that be what he calls the Juganet?'

'That's it. You got it. You got it. That's what he do call 'em!' Tom was highly amused, and chuckled to himself, but Arby was beginning to feel he was perhaps flogging a dead horse.

Jane kept up her enthusiastic interest and pressed him. 'Tom, what else is there besides fire?'

'Well, it's… it's not fire… it's more like burnin' really.'

'Like a rainbow?' asked Arby. 'In the air?'

Tom considered this for a moment then replied, somewhat mysteriously. 'No… It's by the ground, in the air… it's ah, in the stones… You know, it's like one thing inside the other.'

'Can you draw it?' asked Jane.

'Oh yes.' Tom wet his finger and drew in the dust on the floor, a shape resembling an elongated doughnut.

Arby thought hard, but couldn't figure out what it was supposed to mean.

'It's glowing, you see, because of the power.'

'Where is it then?' asked Arby.

Tom thought for a moment and then replied. 'I… well, I forget, you see. I been up there once, but… but they made me forget… up in the 'ospital, they made me forget all those things you see.' Tom looked up sadly. 'But I see it burnin'… I do love fire… but they made me forget.'

Arby looked down at the doughnut shape again. 'And this is what it looks like, is it?'

Tom went into deep sad thought. Then, unable to expand on his vision, he answered sadly. 'Sometimes.'

'It could be a maze,' said Arby.

'Round 'ere?' said Jane.

Arby pointed at the drawing again. 'Is this what you see, Tom, or what Sky sees?'

'That's it,' claimed Tom.

'How big is it?

'Oh, miles and miles.'

'Is it a tunnel, Tom?'

'Yes… yes… Like a wheel going round.'

'I don't get it.' Jane had heard enough.

'Neither do I,' agreed Arby.

Sky then appeared next to them. 'Well?'

Arby shook his head. 'Sorry.'

'Sorry? Is that it?' Sky's tone became angry. 'Tom knows! The only one amongst you to remember what we taught you! Again and again we came, and every time you turned your backs on us, intent upon your own destruction. You have despoiled all the secret places, and chaos is coming again… Sorry, you will say… And you will deserve whatever it is that befalls you!'

At this Tom piped up, singing, 'All things bright and beautiful, all creatures great and small, all things wise and wonderful…' He whispered the last line. 'The Lord God made them all.'

Arby tried harder to figure out what the drawing meant. A maze? A wheel? A coil?

'A tower?' suggested Jane.

It was now early morning, and dawn was breaking. A watery sun between thin cloud brought light to the countryside. Birds began singing their boisterous greeting to the new day.

The Land Rover was parked by a dry stone wall. All four, Arby, Jane, Tom and Sky, were looking up at the majestic sight of Glastonbury Tor. The sheep paths running around the girth of the hill looked exactly like the contour lines in Tom's dust drawing…

Sky stepped forward and took a long look at the magnificent sight before him.

Tom closed his eyes so that he could better catch Sky's thoughts. 'He's lookin… he's waitin'… he's searchin' like… he's happy…' Tom smiled, relieved. Then in a sudden switch of mood he shouted angrily at Sky. 'I gotta go back to the 'ospital… You said I could go back!'

'Go then,' said Sky, resigned.

Tom got back into the Land Rover.

Arby approached Sky. 'No good? That's not it then?'

'There is something there, or the echo of something… The place is in honour of the Travellers… I did not expect this destruction, this desecration… Nothing has any worth, does it?' Sky sounded deeply dismayed and disappointed.

Arby and Jane felt guilty, but were not quite sure what of. Arby was probably the closest to it when he thought of the steady erosion of wild things, and the use of pesticides which were beginning to kill the good along with the bad, but his thoughts were limited by his scant knowledge of the wider world. Still, he felt a share of guilt…

'You mean it's been smashed up or somethin'?' asked Jane.

'I don't know… something has happened.'

'So it's not the Juganet then? You can't get away?' said Arby, glumly.

Sky scanned the place one more time. 'Something is left… but I'm not sure what… I will stay here. You take Tom. Go on. I will call you if I –'

Jane crossed him. 'But you said you mustn't be left,' she said.

'And what about Goodchild?' warned Arby.

Tom leaned out of the cab and shouted irritably. 'Come on. It's cold here. I got to get back to me tea round!'

Sky closed his eyes and said, 'I will call you.'

The Land Rover was being watched from a high vantage

point. It was speeding its way along a country road, way down below. It was Sky's view. He'd spirited himself up to the top of the Tor.

He looked around at the ruined church of St Michael. It was such a part of myth and fable, concerning King Arthur, Joseph Of Arimathea, and the Holy Grail. For some people, it was a way-station on lines of force, ley lines, connecting important religious and mythological sites all over the country. For others, it was a music-driven focus, a magnet for a jumble of vaguely religious-cum-folksy, myth-based cults, and sundry other ancient beliefs, like Druidism – or anything that seemed applicable at the time. Glastonbury was a place to connect with a cool, popular, alternative lifestyle, a haven for drop-outs and those of an anti-establishment persuasion – including anarchists and those who simply didn't want to be part of the established mores of the day – though some would say it was for those people who didn't want to work for some reason or another. Being a hippy, or drop-out, became an occupation in itself, with the somewhat vague philosophy of total equality with everyone sharing... the commune community.

But for Sky, whatever it's power and purpose was originally, it was now spent... useless to him.

Roy had his nose in a book. Several more books surrounded him with titles such as *Secret Britain*, *Riddles in the English Landscape* and *Mysteries of Stonehenge*. He was mugging up on an idea he'd had about Sky's belief that this Juganet might be something from the past that actually did still have some kind of power to it.

His father came in stirring a cup of coffee.

'What's all this?'

'Books,' was Roy's sullen answer.

'I suppose there's no danger of you doing the washing-up, is there?'

Roy declined to answer, but asked him, 'Ever heard of a Juganet?'

The Major's brow furrowed in thought. 'No. Why?'

'Neither has anyone else.' Roy slammed the book shut.

The Major was about to have a go at Roy, but the telephone started ringing and broke the tension. The Major picked it up. 'Four double two six. Major Briggs speaking... Yes, Sergeant, I'll tell them. Just this time, just this once, but in future I –' The line had gone dead before he could make his point. The Major replaced the receiver. 'That's all the thanks you get. Well, they've got one of them.'

'Sky?'

'No, the other nutter.'

On the top of Glastonbury Tor, Sky was still contemplating the gothic tower, trying to feel and understand what residual power still lay within it. His eyes closed in deep thought...

When he opened them, there was a standing figure silhouetted in the arched opening of the ruined porch doorway. He had long, curly hair and wore a brown, blanket-like poncho with several home-made looking necklaces hanging down. The figure was staring intently at Sky. He first bowed, and then knelt in deference before he addressed Sky as... 'Master!'

A short distance from the Tor, down at the town level in a field, stood a tatty looking old caravan. It was in the corner right next to a thick overgrown hedge. The van had obviously seen better days and was now in dire need of a lick of paint and possibly some structural repairs, since it sagged a bit on its axel.

Inside the caravan was a beautiful young woman called Suzannah. She was dressed in what might be termed as 'homespun', all very dun-coloured, woolly and rough – the hippy style, which was the antithesis of 'couture' and was intended as a gesture, a statement, against all thing mass produced.

She and her partner, Michael, had decided to stay in Glastonbury after attending the previous year's open-air Rock Festival. She had been already pregnant at that time and gave birth to a son two months later.

As a young girl she'd led a sheltered life. Neither she, nor her parents, expected her to gain any great results at school, and she duly didn't. She seemed destined for a humdrum existence... until the late Sixties. As a teenager, she rebelled with all the rest and was disowned by her family, because of the way of life she chose to follow. She eagerly became part of the revolution that was taking place. Teens were not just rebelling, they were doing things about peace, protesting about the Vietnam War, promoting an unashamed use of drugs, and generally doing things differently in the arts, music, writing and publishing. Suzannah was completely bowled over by the whole 'peace and love' message of flower power, and was thrilled by the whole existentialist weirdo hippy philosophy.

She had met Michael, a man in a serious search for other believable and valid parallel truths in religion, astrology and myth. She also approved of his ambition to become a maker of rough-hewn, some might say crude, gemstone and pottery jewellery, copies of Celtic designs. Suzannah bought into Michael's dream that he had found the place where it all came together – the Glass Island, as he called Glastonbury. A crossover point, he'd told her, where magical, phantasmagorical things were present. Prophesies, written by Druids and Celtic bards, would certainly come about at that holy place. All they had to do was wait…

But that was in the summer. Then, all was sunshine and flowers and music and laughter and song… But now, with winter approaching, and little or no money coming in, and a child to think of, the edges of Michael's beliefs were starting to fray. In the cold light of day, Suzannah was beginning to realise that Michael's dream of peace, love, freedom and happiness was looking a little hazy. She had no feelings of being liberated… Life, for her was just a hard struggle to cope without the essential wherewithal to do so. The caravan they lived in was a shambles – no water, no sanitation and, crucially, no heating. They lived on hopes. Hopes of a miracle, which may or may not happen…

Suzannah had begun to feel trapped.

She was comforting the crying baby boy, who on Michael's insistence was called after an Arthurian character, Avalloch. The child had become the centre of her life. She loved her baby like no other. Suzannah gently rocked him in her arms, shushing him until he stopped crying. She wrapped a blanket around him and laid him in his cot.

'There, there's a good boy,' she whispered.

The long-haired man that Sky had seen on the Tor, Michael, entered and said in an excited voice, 'Suzannah! He's here.'

She ignored him and continued to settle the baby. 'Michael, I'm trying to get him to sleep, can't you…'

Then he said emphatically, 'I'm sure it's him, the one we've been waiting for.'

Suzannah looked up and was rather surprised when she saw Sky standing next to Michael. 'Oh…'

'I've found him, just like it says in *The Green Book*.'

He reached for a small book, opened it and read from it. 'For no-one shall know where he was born of or from whence he came. This Lord of Anhoun. Him it was who placed the magic beasts in circles to guard holy Avalon. Three times he shall come and three names he shall bear: Keeper of The Grail, Lord Of The Glass Island and at the third coming he shall be Evalake The Unknown… Come to build again the abode of light on the Isle of Glass… You shall seek him and find him in the temple of the stars.'

'Who speaks this?' asked Sky.

'Merthyn. It's from *The Green Book Of Merthyn*,' said Michael excitedly.

Sky held out his hand to look at the book.

Michael placed it on his palm, then approached Suzannah. 'And there he was, my love, up in the chapel.'

'The chapel?' asked Suzannah, uncertain what to think.

'In Saint Michael's Chapel… The temple of the stars. It all fits! This is his third coming.'

He indicated Sky. 'This is Evalake!'

Suzannah looked confused, worried, and not at all happy or convinced.

'Oh come on Suzannah!'

She studied Sky carefully. He was good looking, she

thought, but secretly she worried if he'd ask for lodging, or money even. 'Are you? Are you Evalake?'

Sky concentrated on Michael and probed his brain. He read his mind to try and understand what he was thinking. Sky went over the hotch-potch of wild fanciful concepts, prophesies and half-baked ideas about astrology that the man believed in. Then came to an inevitable conclusion. 'I am not him whom you seek…'

'Not him?' Michael was distraught.

'You are right to believe… It is good that you seek, but you have come too late in the history of your people…'

Outside, with the Tor in the distance towering over them like a sentinel, the wind that always signified Goodchild's presence suddenly began to blow. The field itself, where the caravan stood, started to erupt with green energy – grass, weeds nettles and creepers began to move toward and then cover the caravan, as it came under attack from the living organic things around it. Trees in the adjacent hedgerow, leaves and ivy, all joined in and converged on the caravan…

Inside, they were, as yet, blissfully unaware of what was happening.

'If you're not him, who are you?' asked Suzannah suspiciously.

'I am a Traveller. There have been others, as your book says.'

'It is true then?' said Michael. He was suddenly looking brighter, expecting confirmation of his beliefs. However, he didn't hear what he was hoping for.

Sky spoke with a cruel certainty, using a parable form. 'It is true, but not true. Understand it like this… This place was once a metacentre, what your book calls a 'Holy Island' and there were circles. Not circles of astrological beasts, as you have taken to believe in, but circles of force… Travellers – Gods you called them – visited this place millennia ago. What you read are symbols, or fragments of symbols… The truth that men once saw was like a window of many colours, but now the window is shattered and lies in glittering shards across the floor, so that the fragments you pick up, cannot, can never, be the whole. And then… the wind of chaos begins to blow through the open space…'

Unseen, as Sky was talking, green shoots had entered through the gaps in the panels of the caravan wall and were slowly moving in all directions through the caravan. One tendril was creeping snake-like over the floor and threatening the baby's cot…

'Then it's all wasted?' said Suzannah bitterly. Her outcry reflected all the things she'd had to put up with, and all the sacrifices that Michael had imposed upon her, because of his belief in a crackpot hippy dream of 'The New Religion'.

'You said… Chaos would begin?' said Michael, repeating Sky's analysis. Then he looked at Suzannah, bereft. 'Then there is no point,' he said.

Suzannah was stony faced.

'There will be survivors,' said Sky – as if to placate Michael, after having totally shattered his dreams. 'They are the ones I must help… Not you, not here, not now.'

A window pane smashed through with a loud crash! The vicious wind whipped through the caravan, sending everything that was loose crashing to the floor. Suzannah was terrified. She screamed and rushed to get the baby… as a flailing branch literally grew up through the floor of the caravan. Suzannah avoided it, plucked the baby from his cot and held him close to her.

'Get him out!' yelled Suzannah. 'Michael! Get him out of here, he's evil!'

Michael turned on Sky and jabbed a finger at him. 'Get out! Get out!' Then, he cursed him for good measure. 'Aroint Thee!'

The invasion of organic matter began to get more chaotic and started to move even faster. Finger-like roots quickly took hold of Sky and entwined about him like ivy around a tree trunk.

Sky called to them above the noise of the howling wind. 'There is nothing I can do… this is the Animus…'

More windows crashed and plant life began to take over the interior of the caravan. Then roots start crushing the walls.

High up on Glastonbury Tor stood Goodchild. He was orchestrating the attack on the caravan below, gesticulating and waving in further attacks.

Michael was desperately trying to hack a way out of the advancing greenery with an axe, smashing at the trailing branches that now covered the entire caravan. He was hoping to make a way out for Suzannah and the baby. The situation looked hopeless, but he managed to clear the doorway.

As soon as he opened the door, Michael was confronted

by stronger, thicker branches that began flailing at him. In a corner of the caravan Sky was all but buried in leaves and roots. As a last resort, and with a supreme effort, he raised his hand, palm outward, and tapped into his powers once more. A blast of energy emanated from his hand and… there was silence. The wind subsided, the plant life became still. The attack had ceased.

Michael went over to Sky, who now lay unconscious in mounds of roots leaves and branches.

Suzannah, shielding the baby, screamed, 'Michael! Get that thing out of here. Get it out! Get it out of here!'

In using his powers again, Sky had reached a kind of tipping point. He knew that there was a race on. He would either gain all his strength – or lose out to the forces of the Animus through Goodchild… And if that were to be, Sky would fail in his mission, with the outcome that he would become nothing more than cosmic dust.

Sky's main purpose for that moment was to get free from Goodchild.

He opened his eyes as the leaf mould began to cover him, exposing the image of deep space, and Sky removed himself from the scene…

Sky began calling telepathically. 'Arby! Arby!'

Arby was driving through the countryside in the Land Rover in response to Sky's cry for help. Jane was in the passenger seat, looking out of her window for Sky. She carefully checked any likely-looking spot.

Arby scanned the countryside too. 'He's got to be around here somewhere…'

'I don't know how he expects us to know where,'

complained Jane. 'He just yells "help" and we come running.'

Arby said, 'I say we carry on for another ten minutes and then if we can't find him we go back. OK?'

Jane thought this over and then suddenly yelled, 'Stop! Look. Over there!'

There was a squeal of brakes as Arby pulled to a halt. There, at the side of the road, lay Sky, on a heap of gravel. Jane and Arby rushed over to him.

He spoke to their minds urgently. 'Dark. Hide!'

Jane touched his neck. 'He's as cold as marble. Come on Arby, we've got to help him!'

'Where to?

'Anywhere! I don't know.'

They lifted him and carefully put him into the back of the Land Rover. Arby gunned the accelerator and they went off in search of somewhere for Sky to hide. They passed a sign saying: 'Stanford Park Estate. House For Sale'.

'How about there? Probably empty, don't you think?' said Arby.

Jane was not sure. 'Dunno… s'pose there's somebody there?'

'Oh, too bad. When the devil drives, as they say.'

Arby turned into the gateway of the house, and drove on up the path towards the house. It was an old farmhouse, strangely sited right in the middle of a field, with forest plantations on three sides of it…

Suzannah and Michael were packing ready to move out of the shambles that once was their home. Michael went to pick up his 'holy' books.

Suzannah was still tearful, but absolutely determined now. 'No Michael,' she warned him. 'Not those. Please. I'm frightened of all of it. Yes, all of it.' She looked at the chaos in the caravan, then hurried out of the door with the baby.

Michael took a long, lingering look at the psychedelic picture on the wall depicting the circle of mythical astrological beasts surrounding Glastonbury. He unceremoniously tore it off the wall. Without a backward look, he picked up the baby's basket-weave carry cot and followed Suzannah out of the caravan into the field.

They made their way across the field to the road, with as many belongings as they could carry. The rest of their moveable stuff was piled on to the pushchair. They had started a journey to find a new beginning.

Michael mumbled bitterly. 'I s'pose it's back to bloody teaching...'

Suzannah didn't answer him and just kept her head down.

Invisible to them, an angry Goodchild watched the pathetic sight of the couple. Both utterly disillusioned, but for their own different reasons, perhaps? They passed him to go on up the road, and on to a new, different way of life.

A golf ball rolled along the carpet and just missed a teacup placed on its side. Major Briggs was practicing his putting on the living room carpet when the telephone rang again. He showed signs of annoyance before dropping his putter.

'People must think I've got nothing better to do!'

He picked up the receiver and greeted the caller sharply. 'Hello? Yes. Right... well I'll ask him... Hold on a sec.' He put the phone down and looked through the serving hatch at Roy, who was doing the washing-up. 'They've spotted them. Down around Huntspill way. The Avon and Somerset police want to know if you'd help them out?'

'How exactly, Dad?'

'You know their Land Rover and they seem to think you might be able to suggest some places that tearaway might be likely to hide.' He added, sotto voice, 'And it puts you on the right side of things… get my meaning?'

Roy thought it over. Then decided it had got to be fun. Better than washing-up anyway. He smiled at his dad. And said. 'Sure, I'll do anything I can to help.' Roy quickly dried the cup he was holding. 'On my way.'

Jane and Arby parked the Land Rover by the front gate of the sinister looking, empty farmhouse. It seemed to be incredibly old and dilapidated, plus there was an odd air of Hansel and Gretel about it – in that it looked a tiny bit like it was not made from timber, brick or stone, but of some strange soft-looking substance. There was a 'For Sale' sign in front of the garden, which was just grass with a paved path. They got out of the Land Rover, opened the garden gate, and began a cautious approach up the crazy paving path to the house.

'Funny sort of place,' mused Arby, 'for round here, eh?'

'Not sure I'm 'appy about this Arby… It's weird.'

Suddenly, Jane screamed when, as if from nowhere, a large squawking black crow descended upon them. Jane shielded her head from its flapping wings. The bird flew away.

'Told you, Arby. I don't like it,' Jane said.

'We'll let Sky decide, shall we?' said Arby.

They moved up to the front door. The crow squawked evilly from somewhere behind them... They were becoming fearful of what they'd let themselves in for, yet they continued to edge closer to the porch over the dark-arched, Tudor-type wooden door. Had they bothered to look they would have seen that the wooden porch was made of living timber, with fingers of shoots growing interlaced to form the arch...

Arby was beginning to have second thoughts himself. He went to knock on the door, but as he touched the knocker, he found it was unlocked. The hinges squeaked ominously as Arby pushed the door open...

Chapter Eight
'Life Force'

INSIDE THE FARM HOUSE, they went through the hall and opened a door. They found themselves in a creepy darkened room which, to add to the spooky atmosphere, was full of furniture covered by white dust sheets, giving them a ghostly look…

They kept close together as they ventured into the room. They moved around cautiously…

Jane saw something odd-looking in the gloom. She moved away from Arby to find out what it was and was confronted with a large, ancient-looking, stone-carved sculpture of a crow, covered in trailing cobwebs. It stood at the bottom of a very rickety-looking staircase.

She shied away from it, then came across a dark panelled

door. Despite wanting to get away from this place, her curiosity got the better of her. She decided to open it.

Again, it opened, and again, just like the front door, the opening was accompanied by creaking hinges…

She took a peek inside the next room. It was, by contrast, very bright and airy, but empty. She closed the door and swiftly moved back to join Arby.

'Nothin' in that room,' she said.

Arby drew open a dirty, red curtain and checked out the windows which were covered in dust, so much so, that the window panes looked like opaque glass. When Arby turned back, he looked up and saw a mouldy looking stag's head mounted on the wall. That too was draped in cobwebs.

Jane joined him and looked up at the stag's head. 'They must've left a long time ago. Place is covered in dust an' muck,' she whispered.

'Yeah…' replied Arby, who was seriously considering leaving.

They both heard a sound… It was a bit like a growl. Then silence again…

'What was that?' hissed Jane.

They stood there frozen and began to wonder if they'd imagined it…

Arby moved to close the heavy red curtain, but Jane stayed his hand.

'Don't close 'em all together. Can't see anything.' Jane squinted through the gloom, at something across the room. 'Sky?' she said. She moved towards him. Sky was lying, as if asleep, on a chaise-longue. She bent over his frail looking form. 'How long's he goin' to be out this time?' she complained.

'Looks a lot worse doesn't he?' said Arby, joining her.

'Goodchild?' suggested Jane.

'Bound to be... I told him, we shouldn't have left him at Glastonbury.'

'But he said. He told us to leave him... He doesn't care anyway.'

'He's just usin' us. Like he did poor old Tom,' said Jane.

'Tom wanted to go back to the 'ospital. He was worried stiff.'

Jane shrugged. She found that, however annoyed she became of Sky, when she looked closer at the slumbering star child, the sight of him produced an unexpected emotion in her. A smile crossed her face. 'Just like a baby when he's asleep like that.'

'It's not sleep.'

'What d'you mean?'

'It's just, when he gets like this... When he comes out of it... he seems to sort of... know more. He needs us less.'

Jane wasn't sure about Arby's deduction, and was about to speak when they heard a strange noise, a loud cawing cry from some other room, like a crow.

Jane was petrified. 'What the 'ell was that?' she murmured.

Complete silence as they both listened intently... Then came the unmistakable clack-clack sound of footsteps in the next room.

Arby decided to try and find out who it might be. He followed the sounds and Jane stayed very close to him as he moved towards the door Jane had opened before. To their dismay, the door creaked open of its own accord. They looked into the empty room.

The strange cawing noise came again. Very close by this time.

The sound of the footsteps came closer, and a man stepped into the open doorway. He was, at first, just a dark silhouette against the bright empty room beyond. He paused for a second.

'Yes?' he said.

The silhouette then marched toward them. Now they saw him, he was a short, earnest looking man, with his hands thrust into the pockets of a black three-piece suit which he wore over a black shirt. This, combined with his raven black, oiled, centre-parted hair, made him look rather sinister. However, they immediately felt more at ease when he gave them a bright friendly smile.

'Name's Black. I'm a sort of factotum. Now, we are glad that you could come.' He diverted his eyes over toward the prostrate Sky and then marched toward him.

Arby raced back and stood his ground protectively in front of the strange man.

'But we're sorry to see that the other young gentleman is unwell,' Black continued.

'Don't worry. He'll be alright in a minute,' Arby assured him.

'Very good, sir,' Black nodded.

Jane approached them and rather tentatively asked, 'I… we… hope you didn't mind us coming in… He needs a bit of a rest.'

'We are at your service,' he said with a self-satisfied smirk.

'We?' said Arby frowning.

The man ignored the question.

'Meanwhile, if there is nothing that your young friend requires, perhaps you would like to view the property?'

'You expecting us then?' said Arby confused.

'The land people sir, kindly informed us of your interest. My employer, who sends his apologies, will not be present. Perhaps it would be as well, sir, were I to lead the way?' He backed away toward the staircase and awaited them on the second step.

Jane moved beside Arby.

'What d'you think?' he asked.

'We can't leave him.'

Black called to them from the stairs. 'Your young friend is it? We can absolutely assure you that nothing – untoward – will occur. Please allow me.' He invited them to the stairs with a hand gesture.

Jane and Arby were not sure what to do, but Arby led the way and they followed the strange fellow up the stairs.

On the first landing, he waved an admiring hand at a wood carving in the design of the staircase. 'Please to observe the detail… after Adam,' he explained with a slight smirk. Jane and Arby were none the wiser and followed him up the next flight of stairs.

When they had passed it, the fine 'wood carving' reverted to a gnarled knot of wood…

Their guide reached a dark, cobwebbed landing on the upper floor. He ushered them up to join him. 'Here, the servant's quarters. All long gone now… apart from myself of course.'

Arby had a scary moment when he rested a hand on a banister rail and it snapped off like a carrot and fell down the stairwell.

The man stopped and looked back with a trace of concern on his face.

'Place is rotten! All falling to pieces,' said Jane, pulling back from the banister rail.

'You must understand… Living abroad as we do, certain aspects have sadly deteriorated.' He moved to the end of the landing and opened the bottom of a half-door, like a stable door. He gestured them to go into the room beyond. 'Now. This room has a history… please.' He opened the door just wide enough for them to scramble in.

Arby and Jane found themselves in a scruffy attic room, which was, of course, full of cobwebs.

They looked around for Black.

He was outside the half-door looking in. A sinister smile came to his face as he informed them. 'Unfortunately, I must leave you now.'

He slammed the door shut on them from the outside, and they heard the sound of a bolt being slammed home. They realised with terror that they have been locked in…

On the landing, Black threw his head back and from his mouth came a spine chilling caw-caw-cawing crow squawk…

Sky, now alone, looked very weak and vulnerable lying on the downstairs chaise-longue…

Sure enough, a phantom wind began to blow. It built and built. Dust on the floor started to blow around like a twisting tornado. Then, there came a loud cracking sound as the wall behind Sky split open and a reptilian-like tree root pushed in through the gap.

Sky lay there, seemingly helpless in his stupor. Then a

dark shadow was cast over him. Goodchild stood at the foot of the chaise-longue, glaring down at Sky.

The servant, Black, joined his Master, gave a servile nod and said, 'Everything is arranged.'

Goodchild slipped off his long black cloak and covered Sky completely with it.

Roy had been a bit concerned about Arby and Jane. When he went to see Sergeant Simmonds, to respond to the call for help, he found that there was a police search already in progress.

Not far away from the house, Roy found himself riding in the back of a police Ford Anglia panda car, along with two policemen, PC Bennet and PC Grainger.

The Avon and Somerset constabulary had asked Roy to accompany them on their search for the runaways, hoping he might know of Arby's haunts or at least be able to identify the Land Rover. Roy suddenly felt quite important, being asked to join in a manhunt!

The panda car was driving through the countryside at a steady pace. The constable not doing the driving, PC Bennet, turned to Roy, in the back. 'This other chap? Sky is it? What's he like… not dangerous is he?'

Roy gave this some thought before answering. He'd seen at first hand how easily Sky could knock people out, but he decided to give him the benefit of the doubt, as to whether he was dangerous or merely defensive. He gave an evasive answer. 'I'm not sure… He's certainly delusional. Thinks he's a spaceman or a time traveller or something.'

A snort of laughter from Bennet.

'Mad as a bloody hatter then?' commented PC Grainger,

who was at the wheel. 'I gather he was throwing his weight about down at the school. That right?'

Roy decided not to get involved. 'I don't really know, I didn't get there till after.' He returned to searching the landscape outside.

The car turned a bend and went past a plantation of trees. Roy looked out and spotted something. 'Hang on! Over there! I'm pretty sure that's the Land Rover.'

The police car braked sharply and turned into the track with the 'For Sale' board that had led Arby up to the entrance of the old farm house.

Only now it read: 'For sale. Forty acres of woodland.'

All that could be seen was the Land Rover standing in an empty field. There was no house there at all... Beyond the notice there was nothing but the field and the trees.

The panda car came up and parked next to the Land Rover. Roy got out quickly and checked out the Land Rover. He could see there was no-one in it.

'This is it alright,' said Roy. He touched the bonnet. 'It's still warm. They can't be far off.'

But it was just a field bordered by the two timber plantations. The policemen and Roy looked around the nearby trees, but found no-one.

Roy was intrigued. What was going on? Had Sky just made them disappear? Was this the Juganet? He was pretty well able to believe that anything might be possible, as far as the enigmatic Sky was concerned.

In the locked garret, Arby was trying in vain to get the door open by bashing it with his shoulder. Jane wandered over to the dust-covered window and tried to peer through the glass. She could see nothing. She rubbed on it with her coat cuff, but all she could see was the field outside the house. She backed away, irritably wiping cobwebs off her coat, now really scared.

She urged Arby to hurry up. 'Oh, come on! I don't like this place. I can feel things crawling all over me.'

'It's only cobwebs. Shut up and give us a hand,' came his reply. Arby banged on the door with his fist again.

Jane went back to the window. She managed to sweep some of the dust away from the top of it and looked out. This time she could just about see out of it. And to her utter surprise and delight, she saw Roy and the two policemen.

'Arby!' she yelled. 'It's Roy! Roy's down there… with the police.'

Arby joined her. 'That's great, we'll be alright now,' he said, waving. 'Roy!' he yelled.

Jane joined in, shouting, 'Roy!'

Arby rapped on the window, but they couldn't seem to make Roy hear. 'What's the matter with him? Can't he hear us?' he said.

'Smash it! cried Jane. 'Quick!'

Arby took a run and kicked at the window, but to no avail. It was as if the glass was made of steel. With his second kick, Arby hurt his foot. 'Y-ooow!'

'What's the matter?'

'Damn thing. It won't break!' moaned Arby.

Jane continued to bang on the window and shout, 'Roy!'

Outside, the only sounds Roy was aware of were the singing of birds and the purr of a tractor some way off… Otherwise he could see and hear nothing. He shouted toward the woods at the top of his voice, 'Jane? Arby!' But there was no reply. Roy gazed at the open field in front of the Land Rover and wondered where his friends could have got to...

Constable Grainger came back to join Roy. He gestured at the wooded area. 'I've had a good look around. They could be anywhere, son.' He took out his radio telephone and spoke to the station. 'Foxtrot Lima to control?'

There was a crackle of static. Then an answer came. 'Go ahead, Foxtrot Lima.'

'Yeah, well. We've located Vennor's Land Rover. Right out in a field in the middle of nowhere. No sign of the kids, or the, er, patient. We'll carry on and see what we can see... Oh, you might pass this message on to Sergeant Simmonds. He's got young Vennor's dad with him. Over.'

The controller answered, 'Thank you Foxtrot Lima. Will do. Over.'

Roy was still puzzled. 'Why leave it here though? Right out in the open, where anyone can see it?'

'Why not?' said Grainger.

'Because he always goes for cover.'

'Who's that then?'

'The guy with them.'

'I see... Well, tell you what, you stay here. We'll scout around and meet up with Sergeant Simmonds and Mister Vennor.'

'What do I do if I see them?'

'Give us a shout. We shan't be that far away.'

In their prison, Arby and Jane were still trying to get Roy's attention. But there was still no response. Jane had made her throat sore from shouting so loudly and sat down on the floor next to Arby, who was rubbing his ankle, which was still painful from when he kicked at the window.

'Why can't he hear us?' screamed Jane.

'He didn't even look up,' said Arby. He was becoming increasingly worried.

Then, to cap it all, Jane began to cry.

Arby looked at her wearily, and thought to himself. Oh no! She *would* do this. Girls are all the same. No backbone. He felt obliged to stiffen her resolve. 'Oh pack it in,' he said.

But she continued to cry.

'Jane stop blubbering! It isn't doin' any good is it?'

Arby's angry voice made her stop.

'What we gonna do now then?' she said sniffing.

'All I'm sayin' is crying isn't goin' to help.'

Arby took stock of the situation. They'd been fools to come into the house. Sky should have warned them – and now he was in real danger lying on the couch downstairs…

He made his decision. 'Only one thing we can do. Try calling Sky.' He looked into Jane's face. 'OK?'

Jane nodded.

'Now think… concentrate.' He closed his eyes and bowed his head in an effort to contact Sky telepathically. Then opened them again. 'About time he did something for us.' He closed his eyes again. Arby was in deep concentrated thought, calling to Sky.

Goodchild was being watched closely by his assistant, Black, as he slowly removed the cloak from Sky's body.

Sky was now entwined in a sort of green and silver translucent creeper that was growing over him like lichen.

It was not the usual organic material. It seemed to be something Goodchild had especially created from the Animus to devour his adversary. He was just feeling pleased with his handiwork when, without warning, his mind was invaded by Arby and Jane's calls to Sky.

Goodchild looked unusually concerned. 'They're calling him. Hurry!'

Black moved off and pulled the curtains across, darkening the room.

Goodchild closed his eyes, then chanted, 'Oh, forces of the Earth. Forces from the Earth, forces in the Earth, forces below the Earth. You, who made me manifest, who called me forth from the tree of life, who gave me a voice and this... hated human form... make your will known through me now... against this...' He looked down and held his spread-out fingers over Sky, then continued his incantation. 'Against this abomination. Here we have anathema, alien and evil. Here we have strangeness, unwelcome and unknown. Here we have disease, blastocytic and obscene, spreading its contagion from the diaspora of beyond. Through me, the force of the Animus is gathered. Enclose! Envelop! Smother and... consume!'

He glared hard at Sky now.

Sky's eyes opened. Inside them, the cosmos, the myriad stars, galaxies and nebulae. It would appear that Sky was putting up a fight...

Arby and Jane gave up their effort to contact Sky. They were still trying get out of the upstairs garret.

Arby had gone back to try and open the small, half-door they'd entered by. He wedged a piece of wood in the tiny gap at the bottom of the door to use as a lever. They both hauled on it as hard as they could, but the lever snapped in half. Arby searched the dim-lit room for something else to use, but he could find nothing suitable. He gave up, after giving a final petulant kick at the window.

Arby, too, had lost his spirit. 'It's hopeless...'

They sat down together in despair.

'That's no ordinary door,' complained Arby. 'Or window!'

'If Sky had heard, I know he would have helped,' said Jane, more in hope than certainty.

'Yes,' said Arby flatly.

'This is it then?' Jane said. 'We can't help him, and he can't help us? Maybe, Goodchild has –' She was going to say 'destroyed Sky', but decided not to.

Arby knew what she was thinking, and avoided answering his sister. Instead, he continued looking around the filthy garret for a possible other means of escape. He knew how down Jane was feeling, so he turned to her and said brightly, 'Shall we try again?'

'Try what?

'Sky!' said Arby, trying to sound upbeat. 'I'm sure we'll get through to him this time.'

Jane simply shook her head.

Goodchild was still giving his incantation over Sky. 'Consume! Devour!'

The lichen-like plant was still creeping over Sky but perhaps more slowly now.

A sudden look of rage from Goodchild, as he commanded the Animus, 'Devour!'

But the creeping lichen had stopped… and was in fact gradually disappearing from Sky's face.

Sky now looked Goodchild in the eye defiantly. He then summoned all the power he could.

Black, who stood next to Goodchild, began to look concerned as Sky's hand rose slowly from the organic chains encircling him.

Sky's hand began to glow, not like it had before. This time it has the burning golden light of a sun…

'Master!' said Black in fear of what he saw happening.

Sky then rose up from the couch. He was resplendent, dressed in garments of gold, and now he did indeed resemble one of the ancient gods…

He addressed them, his voice now full of confidence. 'Did you not know? The powers that you have used against me came too late. Now they only serve to make me whole.'

Goodchild and his servant began to back away in fear.

'Now, I am formed… I am, myself.' Sky was suddenly in a standing position, floating just above the couch, with his palm outstretched toward them.

At that moment, Goodchild and his servant were bathed in the golden light which was emanating from Sky's palm. Black made his escape and ran off, leaving Goodchild to face Sky… He shuddered and bowed his head, then retreated under the pressure Sky's new-found power.

'You should have destroyed me earlier… You can never destroy me now.'

Goodchild staggered backwards and out of the door…

'For I have become invulnerable.'

Roy was still waiting out in the cold field, standing by the

Land Rover. He decided to open the driver's door and look inside. He saw a book on the seat, entitled *The Last Whole Earth Catalogue*. He flicked through it, then threw it back into the passenger seat. He noticed that the keys were still in the ignition then got into the cab, and started the engine. He was feeling pretty cold so he put the heater on – which had now been mended by Jane. He smiled at the thought of her mechanical prowess.

He looked around the countryside from inside the cab… Still nothing but trees.

In the garret, Arby was concentrating on forcing a floorboard up to use as another lever. Meanwhile, Jane was at the window.

'The police car's back again,' she said. As she watched, out stepped Vennor. He went to the Land Rover and took over from Roy in the driver's seat. 'Look it's our dad!' she said. 'Dad! We're up here! Can't you see?'

Then she saw the Land Rover drive away.

'No! Dad! No! Come back!' she yelled. 'It's no use now, Arby. He's gone… and Roy's gone now. Why didn't they see us?'

Arby was too concerned about the floorboard to see what happened at the window. 'Well they didn't, so why don't you come here and give us a hand,' he shouted.

Jane joined him reluctantly and helped him pull at the floorboard.

As they struggled to free it, a commanding voice called to Arby. 'Boy!'

They both looked up, to see the alarming figure of Goodchild towering above them…

Jane ran and tried to hide.

However, Goodchild now sounded full of regret and was almost kindly toward them. 'Do not be afraid. You have nothing to fear from me…'

Arby spoke up. 'Why? Who are you?'

'A voice. That is all.'

Arby moved to comfort Jane.

She now faced up to Goodchild. He was just like Sky, she thought, talking in ways they couldn't understand. 'What d'you mean a voice?'

'Once, your ancient forebears worshipped me. But now you no longer have regard. You have ceased to listen to the force that gave you your beginning.'

'What force is that?' said Arby.

'Life itself. I was made manifest, given this form to fight against the alien intruder. Your interference has thwarted that intent… Now, you and your kind must bear the consequence. The alien has made his metamorphosis.'

Arby and Jane got closer together.

'Sky?' asked Jane.

'He is alien,' boomed Goodchild. 'Alien to this world. To this time. To all things living. Now or yet to be.'

Arby piped up. 'We were only helpin' him get away from here.'

'He said we had to help him,' confirmed Jane. 'He's needed, in time to come.'

'There is no need… for… them! No need! Not in this world nor in any world to come. The aliens bring destruction… That is all… That is his purpose…'

Then the echoing voice of Sky intervened. 'No!'

Goodchild recoiled again as Sky materialised before him

in his princely golden robes, No longer did he wear the haunted look he once had. He looked at Goodchild now, with a confidence, a smile and an attitude to match. 'What you call destruction is change. There is need to change… to alter and become.' He looked over at Arby and Jane, who were still cowering in the corner. 'Were it not for me, and the Travellers who came before me, this world would be nothing but a swamp. A mindless, seething swamp. A third rate planet circling your dying sun.'

Goodchild interrupted, holding up his hand. He looked over at the kids. 'Life or destruction… you must choose.'

Sky turned to him. 'The human species has already chosen. They made their choice five million years ago. With the first flint, man bent nature to his will. There can be no turning back.'

'There must be!' bellowed Goodchild. 'Your way, the way of intelligence is the way to destruction! You! *You* made Man take that choice. You made him violate the natural law.'

Sky gave him a superior smile. 'No! Nothing so simple. Humankind has scorned the both of us. The Chaos to come is of man's own making… Neither you, nor I, can help him now.'

Arby was dumbfounded. 'You said you came to help?'

'The survivors Arby… Only the survivors.'

Goodchild said gravely, 'Will you aliens never leave this world in peace? Look around you. Look at the scarred land, the dead water, the ravaged mantle, the poisoned canopy… Whose hand is it? Man! You have made man into an alien, an alien force, throttling life from the surface of his own planet. But the day will come, and soon, when the forces of nature will rebel against the hand of man. That is the true source of Chaos.' Goodchild looked directly at Arby and Jane. 'And you will have caused it… So! Let it begin. Now!'

Goodchild opened up his cloak like bat wings, as if he was about to do something unpleasant to Arby and Jane. Sky held up his palm, which was still glowing and golden, like sunlight. Its power stopped Goodchild in his tracks.

'You may prevent me now, but you cannot escape me forever,' said Goodchild. 'Nowhere will they be safe. Everywhere I will turn the forces of Nature against them.'

'Do so,' warned Sky, 'and you force me to stay in this time to protect them. You know what that means. You can no longer destroy me… and my presence here in this time will cause continual havoc… Is that what you want?'

Goodchild thought this over – and backed down. 'They will be left in peace. Now, go!'

'The Juganet. Tell me where it is and you will be rid of me.'

'It has been destroyed,' said Goodchild with a snarl.

'Where is it?'

'Its power has been absorbed.'

'Where is it?' demanded Sky.

'It is nothing!'

Sky crossed him. 'You lie! The work of the Travellers cannot be destroyed. It is outside time. Where is the Juganet? Where is it?'

Sky blasted Goodchild with glowing waves that penetrated his brain. Gradually, under this pressure, a picture emerged of Goodchild's thoughts. The sun blast on his face merged with the sun rising between the stones at Stonehenge…

Chapter Nine
'The Juganet'

THE HUGE MONUMENTAL BLOCKS of the ancient stone circle at Stonehenge were just standing there, bold, purposeful and utterly magnificent against the horizon… It had been there for at least five thousand years. No-one was really sure of its purpose, or why such a gargantuan effort had been expended to build such a place…

The sun rose, shedding a pale orange light over the misty downland of Salisbury Plain on that cold, bright, Autumn morning. The glistening sunrise was framed between two of the upright stones… just as it had been for millennia… It was an awesome and inspiring sight. Birds were swooping, chirping, flying in and around the stones. A bright day, and all was well with the world… or so it seemed.

*

The peace of this delightful scene was shattered by a powerful whooshing sound! Arby and Jane, transported by some strange invisible power, appeared from nowhere, and found themselves bang in the middle of the inner stone circle.

Jane was the first one to get her bearings. 'Stonehenge! So, you reckon this is the Juganet?'

Arby was unsure and didn't answer her. He moved between the huge sarsen stones.

'Where're you goin'?

'To find Sky.'

'Oh Arby, don't do anythin' daft –'

Jane followed and kept an eye on him as they hurried into the centre of the stone circle.

Then Arby called out, 'Sky!'

Sky was standing on one of the fallen stones, still utterly resplendent in his golden garb. Now, the sun glinting on it making him appear even more godlike. He held his hand up to stop them and said, 'Stay there. You must not come too close.'

'Why?'

'The force is gaining power…'

'This it then? The burning stones? The Juganet?' asked Arby.

'Not the stones themselves, Arby. The force was here long before. The stones only serve to mark the strangeness of the place.'

Arby moved towards Sky.

Again Sky stopped him. 'No.'

'You really are goin' then?' asked Jane. She felt quite

relieved and wondered how she was going to tell her mum and dad about the weird events of the past few days. She decided it would be best to say nothing.

Arby felt let down. He gazed at Sky with sullen face. He'd helped this strange forlorn being from the start without question and now he was going… just like that. 'But you said if we helped you, you'd show us the future.'

'No Arby, it would do you no good… You will all forget what you have learned… It will be as if you had never met me.'

'But we did a lot for you.'

'I know that. Goodbye Arby, Jane. Unlike you, I shall not forget…'

On these words, the whooshing sound started to build, and Sky began to fade and then disappear into a white light.

Arby jumped up on to the stone where Sky had stood and yelled, 'Sky!'

'No, Arby!' cried Jane. Don't go any –'

But it was too late. Arby, just as Sky did, began to disintegrate and disappear into the white light too…

Jane ran up to the stone where he'd stood, calling her brother's name, but she was totally alone among the stones, which now took on a more sinister look. As she stumbled around, trying to get out, she almost bumped into a stone, then backed away from it.

She tried to work out how she'd got there but that thought soon passed away… For her, it was as if she was being guided by an unseen hand.

She turned to go around one of the big stone uprights and

was confronted by Goodchild. He just appeared in front of her, standing by the stones.

He looked at Jane quizzically. 'What do you want? What are you doing here?'

Jane frowned and said, 'Who are you?' The man, she thought, looked a bit frightening.

'Do you not remember?' said Goodchild.

'Remember what?'

Goodchild realised that Jane's memory of Sky had literally been wiped clean from her mind. He began to relax, and spoke to her at just above a whisper. 'It has gone… It has finished… The Earth is free of him.'

'What did you say?'

There was no response from Goodchild.

'My brother. I'm looking for my brother. He came through here. You must have seen him.'

'He came through here you say?'

'Yes.'

'Well he's not here,' said Goodchild. There was the suggestion of a smile on his lips as he turned and sauntered away. 'He's in some other place…'

Jane looked around again and could see nothing. 'What d'you mean? Where did you say? Hey!'

She caught sight of Goodchild going between two of the tall stones and started to go after him. Unseen by Jane, he raised his black cloak at arms length, and disappeared… into thin air.

Jane arrived at the spot where she'd last seen the man. When she looked around, he was nowhere to be seen. 'Hello? Mister?' she called.

She became aware of something by her feet and looked

down… Something was flapping around on the ground. It was a thin black plastic sheet, blowing and flapping in the wind. There was something about it that worried Jane, although it was only a bit of old bin liner or something caught in the breeze. Even so, she backed away from it.

'Jane? Jane?' A voice was calling to her… a friendly voice. It was Roy.

Jane saw him standing at the edge of the stone circle. He was wearing his crash helmet. She made her way to him, smiling with relief. 'Roy.'

'Are you alright?' he asked. He held up a second crash helmet and waved it at her.

She smiled warmly and took the helmet from him.

'I'm on the bike.'

Jane was confused… 'How did you know I was here?'

He smiled at her. 'I don't know… I just… Coming home?'

Jane considered for a second then said, 'Yeah, why not?'

They went off together.

The cloak discarded by Goodchild was now no more than a tattered piece of plastic sack. It flew up into the air and began to dance in the wind, as if caught in a spinning vortex, until it suddenly took off and blew away across the field, where it got entangled and anchored on the jagged rusted spikes of a barbed wire fence… The wind increased, and the black plastic bag ripped and split into trailing finger-like shreds, flapping wildly and pointlessly in the wind…

It had became just one more piece of human detritus…

Chapter Ten
'Chariot of Fire'

ARBY FOUND HIMSELF IN a forested landscape… It looked perfectly normal, and yet he knew there was something slightly odd about it… It was something about the look and, yes, the smell of the place.

The air was crystal clear and there was something scented in the air, like fir tree resin, pitch pine, which reminded him of the desks at his infant school. The trees seemed strange to him, quite unlike the woods he was used to. The trees were mostly of a conifer type, all slightly stunted, and there were rhododendron bushes that over-ran the place, weaving in between the trees. Arby also noted that there appeared to be no defined paths or fields.

He saw smoke rising a short way off and decided to make

his way there, perfectly sure that he would find Sky and sort out all the questions which were forming in his mind – like, is this the future? It hardly seemed much different from his own time…

Arby wasn't even sure this was the future. He'd have expected fantastic changes to have taken place, but this familiar-looking sort of landscape didn't convince him at all.

He knew he had to find Sky, not just to apologise for being such an idiot and following him into the Juganet, but also – if this definitely was some future world – to get some reassurance that he'd be able to get back to his own time. Back to his friends and family…

As he made his way through the trees, he had the odd feeling that he was being watched. Arby looked around several times but saw nothing. He came to a screen of hedges, pushed some branches aside, and saw a small plateau of muddy ground, on which were placed several pyramids of burning sticks. He moved on towards them slowly, keeping an eye out for anyone – or anything. What if there are animals about? Wild animals? he thought with a shudder.

As he approached the fires, he could see that they had been set out in a pattern. Arby wondered momentarily what they were for. There must be someone about, he thought. Sticks don't light themselves. The fires were also the source of the distinctive scent he'd noticed. It was a bit like incense. He decided it would be better to be cautious and try and avoid the fires. He began to move around them and entered a thick stand of trees on one side the fires instead.

Again, the wood he entered seemed so familiar, yet

somehow, unfamiliar. Trees were trees… and yet he knew something was wrong…

After trudging for a while, Arby totally lost his bearings and had no idea which way to go. Every direction looked the same. He suddenly felt very scared and very lonely. He kept telling himself that all he had to do was find Sky. He was sure Sky would help him.

He started to look for Sky again, then saw to his surprise that he was among the trees that bordered the fires again.

'Sky! Where are you Sky?' he yelled.

He felt there was little alternative but to go back to where he'd started. He retraced his footsteps and walked away from the rising smoke. He stopped dead in his tracks when he saw several people, all dressed in raggedy clothes, carrying sticks to put on the fires. He knew he was well within their view, but noted that they were obviously happy to keep themselves to themselves. They seemed to make a point of not looking up at Arby.

Arby was utterly shattered when he heard a loud, commanding voice that sounded very close to him.

'Stranger? Why are you here?'

It so shocked Arby that he slipped and fell on the grass.

'I, Harill, informant of the people, demand to know!'

Arby looked up to find himself facing a man in his sixties. He seemed to be some sort of priest, or authority figure, to the tribe of people. Arby noted that he too was dressed in simple, rough, garments, but he also wore a headband with a sign of some sort at the front and a decorated straw necklace. His eyes bore into Arby as he stared down accusingly over his folded arms.

'Why are you in this place?'

Arby had certainly heard the voice, but the man's mouth had not moved. Arby stood up and took a step backwards. 'I don't know. I don't know how I got here.'

'Stranger. Why do you speak with your mouth?' said Harill sternly.

'Eh?'

'Do you not know? We do not speak with the mouth in the outside world.'

The people who'd been tending the fires now began to creep ominously towards Arby en masse...

Harill raised his hand to stay the approaching people, who were composed mostly of younger men and women.

'Why don't you speak normally?' asked Arby innocently.

Harill's eyes narrowed in rising anger. 'It offends.'

'Who are you?' He gestured to the others by the fires.

'We are the people. And I, Harill, am a servant of the people.'

'What people?'

'The people of the Earth.'

Arby looked around suspiciously and found himself uttering the very same words that Sky had used when they first met. 'What time is this?'

'The time of the cold sun and the sleeping Earth.' Harill looked utterly dumbfounded by Arby's lack of knowledge. 'How can you not know these things?'

'I come from a different time. From 1975. Honestly,' said Arby desperately. 'AD.'

Harill's eyebrows narrowed as he stared at Arby with something bordering on disgust. He started to move slowly and ominously towards Arby, and said with unconcealed authority, 'You must not lie… there is no other time. There is only now.'

The man kept on moving toward Arby until he was close and looking right at him. Arby suddenly realised that Harill's attention was focused on the fur collar of his jacket. Harill gingerly stretched his hand out and felt the fleece. His expression immediately turned to revulsion and disgust at the touch of it.

'What is this?' Harill said.

'It's… it's only a fur collar.'

'Killer!' said the man, retreating speedily.

'What d'you mean?' pleaded Arby.

'It is told. You shall not kill!'

Arby held his collar out for him to see. 'Look, it's nylon. It's only nylon! It's man-made!'

This information made Harill even more outraged. 'Go!' ordered Harill. He pointed to some trees up ahead, which seemed to be covering an opening of some kind in the rocks. 'You are evil! Go! Go to the place of darkness! Go!'

Arby stumbled off through the wood fires, hoping to get away. He had no alternative but to run the gauntlet through the middle of the people who were tending the fires. They started to encircle him, making every effort to avoid touching the 'evil' Arby, while shouting at him in their telepathic voices. The shrill sound of it began to resound in Arby's head. He couldn't think straight and it began to weaken his resolve.

'Go!'

'Go to the place of darkness.'

They kept chanting, with others joining them, until it became a cacophony of shouting voices.

'Go to the place of darkness. Evil! Go! Go! Go!'

Arby staggered through them and ran off into some trees.

He had been running for some time when he stopped to get breath. As he gulped air into his lungs he felt able to continue. He ran on for a while, dodging branches and pushing through bushes. When he burst through a flowered hedge, to his shock and horror, he found himself face to face with Harill...

Arby, in his desperate effort to escape them, realised he'd gone in a circle.

Harill was holding his hand up to stop Arby...

Arby staggered then halted again and the chanting voices began invading Arby's mind once more.

'Go! Go! Evil! Go!'

Harill pointed to the clump of trees again, urging Arby to go there. 'Go to the place of darkness!' he commanded.

Arby followed the direction indicated by the old man at first, then deviated and ran up a slope, trying desperately to get away. He ran on until he found himself in a quiet wooded area full of tall trees.

Arby called out to Sky in his agony. 'Sky? Sky? Where are you? I need you!'

He stumbled close to a tree trunk and two of the ragged tribe people stepped out from behind it, shouting and yelling telepathically. He'd thought he'd got away from them but they seemed to be everywhere in the trees. The blabber of shouting, accusing voices then built into a staccato chant. All the voices at once, chanting together, were now bombarding Arby's brain... He stumbled and tripped as he tried to get away from them. He pressed his hands on his ears, but it made little difference since the shouting was telepathic, from inside his head.

'Go – Evil – Go – Go – Go – Evil!'

Steadily other members of the tribe stepped out from behind bushes and trees. They all stabbed pointed fingers at him as he passed. Their voices merged with the rest into one screaming chant.

'Go-go-go-go-go-evil-evil-evil-evil! Go to the place of darkness.'

Arby made his way painfully over the ridge of trees and tumbled down the other side with no idea where he was headed. He slipped and skidded down over another slope only to find himself in the midst of another crowd of the strange people.

The 'mind shouting' was becoming unbearable for Arby. He began to stagger backwards, obeying their orders. When he stopped, he was faced by a circle of men, including Harill. They were all pointing and shouting at him.

'Go-go-go-go-go! To the place of darkness-darkness-darkness!'

Behind Arby, double doors swung open and revealed a dark, subterranean cave in the rock wall. Another man emerged slowly from the trees and approached Arby. This man too wore a headband, the same as Harill's. He pointed his finger at Arby and through sheer mind-power 'pushed' Arby into the dark space behind a thicket of trees.

Metal doors clanked and locked closed behind him…

Arby came to… silence at last… He peered into the stygian gloom and found himself to be in some kind of concrete building. He was lying on a hard floor at the bottom of a flight of concrete steps, which led to a sort of bridge, again made of concrete. Beyond the bridge, there was a pair of heavy metal doors, similar to the ones at the entrance. They too had wheel locks on them.

It began to dawn on him that the whole place was reminiscent of something he'd seen in magazine pictures one time... It seemed to resemble a missile silo which housed intercontinental ballistic missiles. They had been placed all over the USA as the 'final deterrent'.

He gazed around, looking for a possible escape route, but everything was sealed. Arby was imprisoned in a concrete dungeon... He began to regret very much having followed Sky to this horrible place. He had a growing feeling of helplessness and was beginning to fear the worst – that Sky wouldn't be able to get him back. He suddenly felt a yearning for home, the woods, even for Jane... He bowed his head in sorrow and self pity.

Then he fought against the feeling. This isn't me, he thought. There's bound to be hope. He looked at his surroundings once more. Where was he? Obviously, 'the place of darkness'...

Arby became aware of something behind him. He turned around to find Sky looking down at him, standing there, stock still in all his golden glory. Arby was at last able to relax, now that he felt his rescue was imminent.

'Oh Sky, it's so good to see you. I've been so...' Arby began.

Sky crossed him sharply. 'Why did you come here? You are an alien to this time.'

'So I've found out! What time is this?'

'After the Chaos. The time I was meant for.'

'They the people you came to help?' Arby nodded to the outside.

'They follow my prophesies and think I am one of them.'

'Mmm, you're lucky,' said Arby, as he got up from the floor.

'They are simple people, Arby, not like your complex civilisation.'

'Who are they? Where they come from?'

'They are your descendants.'

'That lot? But they're primitive.'

'You may think so, Arby. After surviving the Chaos, they took another path. They try to live at one with nature.'

'Like Goodchild wanted?'

'Yes.'

'Is that why they called me a killer?'

'Killing is evil to them. They forage for their food and do not force nature to their will.'

'Well they forced me,' he replied bitterly. Arby shrugged his shoulders, indignant at being treated so badly. He wandered away from Sky and found a concrete ledge to sit on. 'Forced me with their minds… Like you did.'

'They are telepaths, that is why they have survived.'

'Don't sound like they need much 'elp.'

Sky moved towards Arby. 'They will stagnate and die out, unless they are led forward.'

'That what you're doing?'

'Yes, these people, simple as they may seem, have far more chance than the people of your time… to reach out, beyond the stars.'

'To be like you, you mean?'

'Yes. It is the destiny of all intelligent beings to stand outside space and time.'

Arby thought this over. 'Well, where did our lot go wrong?'

Sky took a long hard look at Arby. 'You do not reach the stars with rockets. No more than you invent radio by shouting at the sky… You believe in machines, in forcing nature to your will, changing things that have no need to be changed… and that is not the way… What you see here is but a beginning. My message to them is that a single brain has unimaginable powers. Imagine that power expanded and developed by millions of brains… all telepathically linked, and all to one purpose… what need of physical energy then? That is all I can tell you.'

Arby looked around at the bleak grey walls and a shudder went up his spine. He was suddenly frightened. 'Hey? Can I get back, Sky? Can you get me back?' Arby looked into those impenetrable, dark eyes, and he was overcome by Sky's power, dropping into a trance-like state.

Arby awoke on a dilapidated old, recliner couch. He found that he was restrained hand and foot. The people of the future he had first encountered outside were all standing around him in a circle.

The silence was broken when one of them struck a gong. Harill approached, carrying a kind of headdress of ferns, rushes and flowers, and slow-marched forward to take up a position with his back to Arby.

Arby's heart began to race. This – ceremony? – looked a bit ominous, especially since he seemed to be the focus of it all.

Then, a man who seemed to be a high priest of some sort – the one who had 'pressed' Arby into the place of darkness – moved in a deeply respectful manner up towards Harill.

Harill was holding the ornate headdress ready for the approaching man. Then, ceremonially, in an act rather similar to the crowning of a monarch or cardinal, he placed the crown on the man's head.

This done, the high priest turned and addressed the assembled people telepathically.

'Sky, the master man, the one foretold by the prophets, tells us that in the place of darkness, we must speak with our mouths, in the old way.'

The people around the altar stretched their mouths in preparation for spoken-word speech. This was followed by strange sounds, like an orchestra of voices tuning up.

Arby looked around in dread of what might be going to happen. Then he heard the comforting voice of Sky in his head.

'Arby, do not be afraid. What follows is all these people remember and despise of your race's vain, wasteful attempts to reach the stars… I must not interfere.'

The old man, who was the high priest and guide to his people, started speaking with his mouth. 'Peepa of a erff – drive outa a evah, wid a evah!'

Arby was amazed by what he heard – it was hardly speech as he knew it.

The priest indicated a chimney-like area with pipes and the metal wheeled locking mechanism…

The gong was struck again.

The congregation all shouted as one, 'Nahza!'

This gave the whole ceremony a creepy feel for Arby.

He struggled with his ties, but couldn't get loose.

The high priest now raised his arms and called out, 'Misha gontra!'

'Misha gontra. Nazah!' was the response from the congregation.

'Misha gontra!' shouted the priest.

'Nahza – Nazha – Nahza!' came the response.

The priest addressed them, in a kind of prayer with responses.

'In begin was ah stahz…'

'Nahza!' responded the congregation.

The gong was hit again, and continued to punctuate each line of the responses.

'Came ah satalighta.'

'Nahza!'

'Wasa ca ka-navarra.'

'Nahza!'

'An a polla.'

'Nahza!'

'Ca – ka-navarah!'

'Nahza!'

'Nahza wa-ha livtoffa!'

The high priest raised his arms high… Doors slid back behind the dais and revealed an empty shell of a room. The priest's helper then pushed the couch, which was on castors, into the open space…

The high priest accompanied the couch. They moved into the chamber over a bridge, which had a shallow gully running down through the centre of it. This led to a conical structure. The high priest raised his hands over Arby and delivered an incantation. 'Misha gontra. Misha gontra!'

Arby was wheeled forward into the strange structure. The sound of the worshippers chanting in the background got louder.

'Nahza! Nahza! Nahza! Nahza!'

Arby noticed the door of the conical structure. It had the appearance of having been built by schoolchildren! Arby realised that the shape had a very vague resemblance to the command module of a Saturn 5 rocket, used on the Apollo missions. But this one, instead of metal, was all bamboo sticks, tree bark, odd bits of plaited straw, leaves and pieces of cloth. The door closed behind Arby…

The high priest spoke louder, above the chanting voices. 'Misha gontra!' He paused then he thrust his hands in the air, shouting, 'Liftuffa!

The worshippers joined in. The gong was being struck in time with the chanting, which gave a frightening edge to the proceedings for Arby.

'Liftuffa! Liftuffa! Wa ha Liftuffa!'

The high priest, still with raised hands, moved back to the congregation.

Arby, tied to the couch inside the 'rocket', took stock of his surroundings and noticed that the dome structure above him was made of wickerwork and that some ancient looking, dented and dust-covered bits of electrical and computer equipment had been randomly scattered about the place.

He turned to see Sky facing him.

'What's this?' asked Arby.

'I told you.'

Arby looked around at the structure with disdain and even managed to conjure up a sad joke. 'It'll never bleed'n fly!' But he soon lapsed into fear and apprehension about what was to befall him.

Sky continued, 'As I told you. It is what they remember of your technological folly.'

'Hmm? What do they think it's gonna do?'

'They believe in man, not in the machines he makes, nor in the things the machines make. Machines devour… consume, lay waste, and wreck the balance and the harmony that man should live in with Earth.' Sky looked at Arby and added poignantly. 'Or so they believe.'

Arby was confused by Sky's ambivalence. 'Why they build it then?'

'To remind themselves of the road to chaos such things represent. To them, this was your ultimate folly, and they despise you for it.'

Arby became thoughtful for a second, then turned to Sky. 'And you? What do you think?'

'It was a cul-de-sac. A fifty thousand year cul-de-sac that ended with the Chaos. But as you must know, that is a mere speck of time in this planet's history. These people follow a better path.'

'OK, they probably do, but what about me? I can't get back in this!'

'No… Of course not.'

'So what's it for?'

Sky considered before answering. 'They… will burn it.'

Alarm bells went off in Arby's head. He felt distinctly uncomfortable. He remembered seeing a film called *The Wicker Man*, where a man was burnt as a sacrifice…

*

Outside the 'capsule', the high priest was overseeing a man pouring oil into the gully running down the centre of the bridge… His work was accompanied by the sound of the gong and the congregation shouting, 'Nahza! Nahza!'

The high priest made a cross with his arms for the chanting to stop…

There was silence.

Then the priest continued alone, 'Misha gontra… Cantadahna… Tenna, nahna, eida, sehana, siss, favah…' He turned to another helper who held a flaming torch. 'Nissun!'

The man touched the oil trail with the torch.

The priest continued, 'Fouah, ree! Tooah unna. Liftoffa!'

The flame spread rapidly across the bridge to ignite the 'capsule'…

Arby was petrified as he realised what was about to happen to him. As tongues of fire started to consume the capsule, he yelled out at Sky, in desperation, to help him. 'Sky! Help me please! Help!'

'Arby, place your hand on mine…' Sky offered Arby his flat hand. The palm was black and studded with stars. 'You alone will not forget. Take something of these people to your time.'

Arby pressed his hand on to Sky's. After a few seconds, he pulled it away and looked at it with some apprehension…

'Begone!' ordered Sky.

With that Arby disappeared, leaving Sky to carry out his destiny…

*

Arby found himself alone in the kitchen at the cottage. He was a little confused, holding his hand as if it had received an injury of some kind. He rubbed his right palm with his left thumb, almost as if he was trying to get a paint stain off it.

He moved over to the kitchen worktop and picked up the electric kettle. He seemed to be mesmerised momentarily by the shine of it.

He moved across to the sink, picked up a squeezy bottle of washing-up liquid and squirted a few drops into the sink. His attention then turned to the taps, he turned one on, then put his hand into the sink… He was in deep, serious thought as he picked up the foamy soap suds made by the detergent.

He continued to appear ill-at-ease when he moved to the washing machine and looked at the clothes being churned over and over inside it…

The spinning stopped. Arby looked around the room. He then went to a cupboard. There was a transistor radio on it. He picked it up and turned it on, then twisted the tuning knob and got a range of radio static and foreign voices, until he settled on a group singing a pop song…

He gazed around the room again, still deep in thought, when the door opened. In came Jane and Roy. Jane shed her coat and, hearing the music coming from her radio, she snatched it from Arby.

'What are you doin' with my radio?' She walked away with it. 'Break it doin' that. What a row!'

Arby was still not quite sure what was going on. He still seemed somewhat distracted. 'It'll be alright,' said Arby.

'When d'you get back anyway?' asked Jane.

'Just.'

Roy, meanwhile, was looking through the local paper. 'Hey Arby, there's another shoot on Saturday.'

Instead of enthusiasm from Arby, he shot a scowl at Roy. Roy registered Arby's displeasure. What was eating him? he wondered.

'Shoot?' said Arby.

'Yeah, shooting pheasants, you coming?'

Arby frowned and searched for an answer.

'What?'

Jane pushed him aside and started grating some cheese into a bowl. Arby watched her closely.

Something worried Jane. 'I'm doin' sandwiches, you want one? Cheese, or there's some ham if you like...'

A troubled look crossed Arby's face. 'No, no thanks. Not ham...'

'No? Not like you to refuse Yate's best. What's the matter Arby?'

'Nothin'...' said Arby.

'You coming then?' said Roy impatiently.

Arby thought for a few seconds... then grinned and was himself again. 'Well, yeah. If they'll have me. After what happened last time.'

Roy looked at him quizzically. 'What's that then?'

Jane shook her head, surprised, then looked over at Roy for confirmation. 'Nothin' special happened last time... did it, Roy?' she said.

'I only got me a bird, didn't I?' He mimed shooting a shotgun. 'Bang!'

'Oh, regular sharp shooter now, eh?' said Jane.

'No, nothing other than that. Just a normal shoot. Why?'

Arby smoothed his palm with his thumb again. 'No… S'pose not. Not if you don't remember,' he replied.

He turned away from them and looked down at his palm… It had the same fathomless black window into the cosmos in it… just like in Sky's. He slowly closed his hand into a fist…

Arby smiled to himself. It was Sky's gift to him…

He then turned to Roy and Jane full of enthusiasm.

'Saturday? Yeah, why not? Make a few quid too, eh?'

Arby was consumed by a kind of grace, that he'd been given such a gift by Sky. He didn't yet know how he would use his gift… but he'd think of something.

ALSO AVAILABLE
FROM FANTOM PUBLISHING

Raven
by Jeremy Burnham & Trevor Ray

The ancient underground caves were in danger – they were
going to be filled with atomic waste. But forces were at work
to save the sacred ground – forces from another time.
Why did the caves contain mysterious symbols and how did
the legend of King Arthur connect with them? What power
did Professor Young, the archaeologist, have to save the cave
complex? And why did the Merlin suddenly appear?
Raven, on probation from Borstal, found himself caught up
with these strange powers, and began to realise that the future
of the caves depended on him...

Hardback RRP: £14.99 ISBN: 978-1781961148

Children of the Stones
by Jeremy Burnham & Trevor Ray

Adam Brake, a professor of astrophysics, and his teenage son
Matthew, arrive in Milbury, an English village surrounded by
a stone circle. Adam has been commissioned to investigate
the residual magnetism of the stones, but he and Matthew
soon begin to realise that this is no ordinary village…
Based on the classic television series starring Gareth
Thomas and Freddie Jones, this is the original novelisation,
published for the first time in 35 years.

Hardback RRP: £14.99 ISBN: 978-1781960875